PAPERCUTZ™

MORE GREAT GRAPHIC NOVEL SERIES AVAILABLE FROM
PAPERCUTZ™

THE SMURFS #21   **BRINA THE CAT #1**   **CAT & CAT #1**   **THE SISTERS #1**   **ATTACK OF THE STUFF**

ASTERIX #1   **SCHOOL FOR EXTRATERRESTRIAL GIRLS #1**   **GERONIMO STILTON REPORTER #1**   **THE MYTHICS #1**   **GUMBY #1**

MELOWY #1   **BLUEBEARD**   **THE RED SHOES**   **THE LITTLE MERMAID**   **FUZZY BASEBALL #1**

HOTEL TRANSYLVANIA #1   **THE LOUD HOUSE #1**   **MANOSAURS #1**   **THE ONLY LIVING BOY #5**   **THE ONLY LIVING GIRL #1**

papercutz.com
Also available where ebooks are sold.

6: "Hurricane Maureen"

Story
Cazenove & William
Art and colors
William

PAPERCUTZ™

New York

*To Wendy and Maureen, my two
beloved tornadoes. Thank you to
Olivier and Christophe for their trust
and their talents, as well as to the
whole "Bamboo Team" always the
best. You do a terrific job.
And thank you, readers young and
old, for your loyalty.
I dedicate this comicbook to all nature
lovers.*
—William

Maureen: *Hey, Wendy, do you like
your tree¿*
Wendy: *What kind of question is
that¿ Of course I like it!*
Maureen: *And you never fight with
it¿*
Wendy: *LOL... No, but it's a good
confidante, you know¿!*
Maureen: *Ah, and what do you
"confidant" to your tree¿*
Wendy: *Everything you'd really like
to know but never will... Heh heh!*
Maureen: *Phooey, too lame!*

The Sisters #6 "Hurricane Maureen"
Les Sisters [The Sisters] by Cazenove and William
Originally published in French as Les Sisters *tome* 11 *"C'est Dans Sa
Nature"* and *Les Sisters tome* 12 *"Attention Tornade"*
© 2016, 2017, 2020 Bamboo Édition

Story by Cazenove and William
Art and color by William
Cover by William
Translation by Nanette McGuinness
Lettering by Wilson Ramos Jr.
Special Thanks to Catherine Loiselet

For information address
Bamboo Édition:
290 route des Allogneraies
71850 Charnay-Lès-Mâcon cedex FRANCE
bamboo@bamboo.fr – www.bamboo.fr

Papercutz books may be purchased for business or promotional use.
For information on bulk purchases please contact Macmillan
Corporate and Premium Sales Department at
(800) 221-7945 x5442

Managing Editor – Jeff Whitman
Jim Salicrup
Editor-in-Chief

PB ISBN: 978-1-5458-0495-7
HC ISBN: 978-1-5458-0494-0

Printed in India
September 2020

Distributed by Macmillan
First Papercutz Printing

THE DAY YOU WERE BORN, **MAUREEN**, I HAD A GREAT IDEA...

I PLANTED A TREE FOR YOUR BIRTH...

YOU'LL GROW UP TOGETHER.

I PUT IT RIGHT NEXT TO THE ONE DAD AND MOM HAD PLANTED FOR ME...

TOO CUTE!

I TOOK CARE OF IT...

I WATERED IT EVERY DAY...

PSHHHHH

OVER THE YEARS, I NEVER FORGOT IT.

SPLOOSH

IT WAS A GREAT IDEA, RIGHT?!

SO, OKAY, IT NEVER GREW...

BUT I SWEAR I DIDN'T KNOW IT WAS PLASTIC.

5

CAZENOVE & WILLIAM

THIS ONE HERE?

IF THAT'S WHAT I SAID, MAUREEN...

NO... YOU'RE SURE?

DAD AND MOM PLANTED THIS PLUM TREE WHEN I WAS BORN. DO YOU SEE HOW BEAUTIFUL IT'S GOTTEN?

SERIOUSLY?

WOW!

IT MUST BE REALLY OLD!

HELLO? I'M NOT A MUMMY EITHER.

"I CAN'T BEE-LEAVE IT." IT WAS BORN BEFORE ME?!

AH, YUUUP! IT'S KNOWN ME LONGER THAN YOU, SISTER.

SO LUCKY, HAVING YOUR OWN TREE.

I'M SOOO JEALOUS.

BIBILLI BIP...

AH, THAT'S SAMMIE. SHE'S PICKING ME UP.

I'M LEAVING, SHRIMPS.

HMM HMM!

QUICK, LULU, BEFORE WENDY COMES BACK...

WHAT'RE YOU GOING TO DO?

IF WE FIND THE TREE'S PRIVATE DIARY, WE'LL LEARN TONS ABOUT MY SISTER'S SECRETS.

HA-HA! GOOD POINT, MAUREEN!

6

CAZENOVE & WILLIAM

HEY, YOU LITTLE BRAT! WHAT DO YOU THINK YOU'RE DOING?

STRP

EURK!

DO I HAVE TO SAY IT TO YOU IN MAUREEN-SPEAK? THAT SHRUB WAS PLANTED WHEN I WAS BORN! WE'RE CONNECTED TO EACH OTHER... THAT MEANS: **DON'T TOUCH, SISTER!**

MEH, OKAY. I DON'T CARE ABOUT YOUR DUMB TREE!

AND I'D BETTER NOT CATCH YOU HERE AGAIN.

NO, NO, NO... THAT FOOTSTOOL WAS BOUGHT WHEN I WAS BORN...

IT'S MINE! STOP TAKING MY THINGS!

THAT'S A NEW ONE.

THAT GOES FOR THE REMOTE CONTROL, TOO.

AND EVEN THE TV... THEY'RE THE SAME AGE AS I AM, WHICH LINKS THEM TO ME.

SO DON'T TOUCH!

GRUMBL.

AND PRESTO!

I WAS THERE WHEN THESE PANCAKES WERE BORN, SO DON'T EVEN TRY TO TOUCH THEM.

CAZENOVE & WILLIAM

FINALLY... SUNSHINE...

I LOVE SPRINGTIME!

EVERYTHING'S BUDDING...

THE FIRST FLOWERS...

ALL THE SCENTS...

CRITTERS AND BUGS...

FAT WORMS...

AND FRESH MUD...

UUHHH... MOMMY... ARE YOU 100% SURE WE'RE SISTERS?

BECAUSE, WE'VE GOT MORE AND MORE DOUBTS ABOUT THAT.

CAZENOVE & WILLIAM

COME HERE... I'VE GOT SOMETHING URGE-IMPORTANT TO SHOW YOU...

LOOK HERE, WAI--MAUREEN...YOU CAN SEE I'M--⇒PFFF⇐... UGHHH!

THERE! YOU TOLD ME WE'D KNOW WHEN SPRING WAS HERE BECAUSE THERE'D BE POSSUMS ON THE TREES IF WE TOOK GOOD CARE OF THEM.

IT'S BLOSSOMS, NOT POSSUMS!

YES, HEE-HEE. IT'S LIKE THOSE BLOSSOMS I SEE ON YOUR TREE HERE.

OR ON THE ROSE BUSHES. IT'S LIKE THAT, TOO.

YES, BRAVO. YOU CAN RECOGNIZE BLOSSOMS. NOW MAY I GO BACK TO WHAT I WAS DOING?

FIRST I WANT TO SHOW YOU SOMETHING 'STRAORDINARY.

PHOOEY...

COUNT TO TEN...

SO... THEN HOW DO YOU EXPLAIN THIS?

I'VE BEEN WATERING MY BED AND RUBBING DIRT ON IT FOR MONTHS...

...BUT THERE'S NOT A SINGLE BLOSSOM THERE. NOTHING, NADA.

YET IT'S MADE OF TREE WOOD, RIGHT?!

⇒HMMMPH⇐... I REALLY NEED TO MOVE TO ANOTHER PLANET.

FERTILE SOIL

CAZENOVE & WILLIAM

REALLY?

IF THAT'S WHAT I SAID.

OOOH, THAT'S SO COOL, MOM!

?!

MEETOO... MEETOO...

I WANT TO REPAINTINGIFY THE WALLS IN MY ROOM.

SCR... EEEEEEEEE

OKAY, MAUREEN.

FOR REAL?

HUH?

IF THAT'S WHAT I SAID.

SO GREAAAAT!

I'M GOING TO REPAINTINGIFY MY ROOOOM...

IT WILL BE THE PRETTIIIIEST...

LALALALEEEEEREE

MOM, IF YOU LET MAUREEN DO IT, IT'S GOING TO BE A DISASTER. WE'LL HAVE TO REPAINT THE WHOLE HOUSE AFTERWARDS... THE NEIGHBORHOOD, IN FACT.

DON'T WORRY, WENDY, I'M NOT FINISHED.

MAUREEN, DO YOU KNOW WHAT YOU HAVE TO DO BEFORE YOU PAINT?

UUUH... OPEN THE CAN?

YES, OF COURSE. BUT YOU ALSO HAVE TO SORT THROUGH YOUR THINGS AND YOUR TOYS, EMPTY ALL YOUR FURNITURE SO YOU CAN MOVE IT...

...DO A THOROUGH CLEANING, TAKE DOWN ALL YOUR POSTERS, FILL THE HOLES IN ALL THE WALLS...

HMMPH...

LATER...

SO, YOU DON'T MIND THAT YOU AREN'T REPAINTING YOUR ROOM?

OH, NOT AT ALL, NAT...

IT'S MUCH MORE FUN TO WATCH WENDY DO IT. HEE-HEE!

OOF! NNGH!

CLOTHES

CAZENOVE & WILLIAM

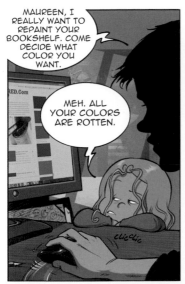
MAUREEN, I REALLY WANT TO REPAINT YOUR BOOKSHELF. COME DECIDE WHAT COLOR YOU WANT.

MEH. ALL YOUR COLORS ARE ROTTEN.

I WANT RED. IT ISN'T COMPLICATED.

THERE'RE LOTS OF REDS FOR YOU. LOOK!

WHAT? THAT'S RED? HOOONESTLY. I DON'T WANT THAT RED...IT'S LAME!

CALM DOWN. WE'LL FIND WHAT YOU WANT...

JEEZ! THERE ARE LOTS OF SHADES OF RED!

GARNET

CHERRY RED

CARMINE

SCARLET RED

GRENADINE

VERMILLION

TOMATO

CRIMSON

GRIM SUN? YUCK, DISGUSTING.

LISTEN, IF THESE DON'T SUIT YOU, SHOW ME WHAT YOU WANT.

WENDY...

WENDY...

WENDY...

THIS MORNING, WHILE YOU WERE TAKING A SHOWER, YOU KNOW, I FORGOT TO TELL YOU...

...I DROPPED YOUR SMARTPHONE IN THE TOILET... IT DIDN'T BREAK, BUT THERE'S LOTS OF WATER IN IT...

AND IT STINKS A LITTLE BIT.

⸘ARRGHL⸘... AH, GOOD. THERE, SEE, DADDY...

...THAT'S ZACTLY THE RED I WANT.

HEE-HEE

CAZENOVE & WILLIAM

POM POM
PO
POM
POM PO

DE BEAUX MOMENTS

HERE, MAUREEN, PUT THESE IN THE HALLWAY, PLEASE.

WHAT? YOU'RE GOING TO TAKE EVERY- THING OUT?

YES, OF COURSE. I HAVE TO MOVE OUT ALL THE FURNITURE...

...SO I CAN PAINT BEHIND THEM, YOU SEE?!

HERE YOU GO. HERE'S THE NEXT BATCH.

GOT IT, BOSS.

WITH THE OTHERS IN THE HALLWAY?!

YOU CATCH ON QUICKLY!

I'LL GIVE YOU THESE, TOO.

COOL!

THESE, TOO, AND THAT'LL DO.

DITTO. PUT THEM IN THE-- UH...

MAUREEN?

HEEEEY. STOP READING MY PRIVATE DIARY!

THEN YOU SHOULDN'T HAVE GIVEN IT TO ME.

CAZENOVE & WILLIAM

WENDYYY... THERE'RE SOME WEIRD THINGAMAJIGGIETHINGIES ON YOUR TREE...

IT MUST'VE CAUGHT A BUG, SOME KIND OF TRUNK COLD.

LOL! STOP YOUR BABBLING.

OR THE NEIGHBOR'S CAT DOESN'T LIKE IT.

ACTUALLY, I USE IT LIKE MY PRIVATE DIARY...

FOR EXAMPLE, IF I HAVE A FIGHT WITH *MASON*, I MAKE A NOTCH. WHEN IT'S WITH YOU, THAT'S THREE LINES... IF I HAVE A FUN DAY WITH *SAMMIE* OR *EMMA*, BINGO! TWO MARKS.

BUT IT'S EXTRA CRUEL TO MAKE HOLES IN A TREE. YOU'VE GOT NO RIGHT TO DO THAT!

THEY'RE NOT HOLES.

THEY'RE NOTCHES...

AND ONLY ON THE BARK. IT DOESN'T FEEL ANYTHING.

YOU KNOW NOTHING ABOUT WHETHER ITS BARKING'S FRAGILE.

HEEEEELLLP... MY SISTER'S A TREEEE TORTURER!

LATER...

AH, YOU HAD ANOTHER FIGHT WITH YOUR SISTER, RIGHT?

MMMM... ⸲YUMMMMPFFFR⸳... THREE TIMES!

GRUMPF...

13

CAZENOVE & WILLIAM

WENDY... WENDY...

YOU HAVE TO HELP ME FIGURE OUT SOMETHING.

HEY! THAT REALLY SOUNDS IMPORTANT...

WHAT DOES *"PLIGIBULL"* MEAN?

PLIGIWHAT?

WHERE DID YOU READ THAT WORD?

IN A GRAPHIC NOVEL I HAVE IN MY ROOM.

THERE'S A SPOT WHERE THERE'S A GUY WHO SAYS, "WELL, I'M REALLY GOING TO PLIGIBULL..."

AND IN A MOVIE, THEY ALSO SAY IT...

PLIGIBULL PLIGIBULL PLIGIBU...

OH! OH, YES! I KNOW WHAT THAT MEANS. IT MEANS YOU'RE GOING TO GET IT!

ACTUALLY IT WAS A TRAP... WENDY INVENTED THAT WORD AND WROTE IT INTO HER DIARY TO PROVE I'D READ IT.

THAT'S WHY I'M GOING TO LEARN ALL THE WORDS THAT EXIST. THAT WAY I WON'T FALL FOR THAT AGAIN.

OKAY... WE'LL START WITH THE LETTER "A."

CAZENOVE & WILLIAM

WOO-HOO!

A TREE IS A REAL PLAYMATE.

IT CAN BE A SWING...

HIGHER... HARDER..

AND ALSO A TREE ADVENTURE PARK.

TUNK
TUNK
TUNK!

IT'S ALL GOOD. I'VE GOT IT.

THERE'S DODGEBALL, WHICH I TOTALLY ADORE.

TANK

KA

PA

ON THE NOSE!

AND BAM! MEGA HEADER SMASH.

BUT MY FAVORITE GAME OF ALL TIME IS TO PLAY JUNGLE GIRL.

OYOYOOYOOOOOOO OYOYOOOOOO OOOO...

THE SNAG IS THAT WENDY DOESN'T WANT ME TO TOUCH HER TREE.

MMPPFF...

WELL, HAPPY FAMILIES IS A FUN GAME, TOO.

MYEP, MEH. I'M NOT SURE THE TREE LIKES IT.

YUP, THAT'S THE THIRD TIME IT'S MISSED A TURN.

CAZENOVE & WILLIAM

SO, WHAT DID YOU END UP PLANTING?! FRUITS AND VEGGIES?!

THAT'S RIGHT! YES, A LITTLE OF EVERYTHING.

YOU DID IT PROPERLY AND FOLLOWED ALL THE STEPS?

YOU KNOW, LIKE WHEN I EXPLAINED IT. BUT YOU WEREN'T LISTENING TO ME.

YEAH, YEAH...

FIRST, DIG A DEEP ENOUGH HOLE...

THEN DROP IN THE SEEDS...

COVER IT, MIXING A LITTLE FERTILIZER IN WITH THE DIRT...

AND THEN WATER IT. YOU DID THAT, TOO?

YEAH, BUT...

OF COURSE, WE DIDN'T FORGET ANYTHING... DO YOU TAKE US FOR A BUNCH OF AMATEURSIES OR WHAT?!

OKAY, WELL, FIGURE IT OUT YOURSELF. AH... I CAN'T TELL YOU ANYTHING, YOU LITTLE PITBULL.

YOU'RE THE "PITBALL," SO THERE!

APPARENTLY, IT'S JUST THE SEEDS YOU'RE SUPPOSED TO PLANT, LULU.

YOU'RE SURE?

CAZENOVE & WILLIAM

SO, WENDY, DO YOU KNOW WHO YOU'RE GOING TO ASK TO HELP PAINT YOUR ROOM?

HMMM... ACTUALLY, I'VE GOT THREE OPTIONS...

MASON, YOU, OR MY SISTER.

YOU'RE COMPLICATED!

THE PROBLEM WITH MASE IS THAT HE'S TOO SLOW. I'LL BE RETIRED AND HE WON'T HAVE FINISHED HIS WALL.

PLISH PLISH

WITH YOU, IT WOULD BE EXTRA GREAT AND SUPER-FAST.

I TRUST YOU 200%.

HEH HEH, WHO'S THE BEST?

~AAARGH!~... BUT, BUT WHAT HAVE YOU DONE?

WITH MAUREEN, IT WOULD BE A REAL DISASTER.

IT'S NOT MY FAULT! THEY THREW THEMSELVES ONTO ME...

AND THAT WOULD WIND UP A MEGA BRAWL, FOR SURE...

TAKE THAT!

MWAH HAHA!

SO THEN... WHO DO YOU CHOOSE?

MY SISTER!

IT'LL BE A TOTAL BLAST.

CAZENOVE & WILLIAM

READY TO REDECORATE EVERYTHING, SHERIFF WENDY?

LET'S GO!

Woo Woo Woo

CLOP

⋛SNURF, SNURF, SNURF!⋚ PE-EW! WHAT'S THAT SMELL? YOUR PAINT STINKS!

OKAY, WHAT?

WHAT'D I SAY?

WHY DID YOU BRING ME TO YOUR SISTER'S ROOM?

WE'RE GOING TO REPAINT IT, TOO?!

HERE.

MAUREEN'S MR. BUN BUN? HOW COME?

SNURF SNURF

HUNMPFF...

THE INCRE

THAT'S STINK!

WHEW KOFF KOFF KOFF KOFF KOFF

YOU'RE RIGHT.

ARGH

YOU'RE RIGHT.

GASP GASP GASP

18

CAZENOVE & WILLIAM

WOOOW! IT'S *SOO* PRETTY, WENDY!

YOUR ROOM'S SO WELL PAINTINGIFIED!

I HAVE TO ADMIT.

WE DID A GOOD JOB!

I'M GOING TO HELP YOU PUT YOUR FURNITURE BACK.

OOF!

NO, NO, NO. WAIT, MAUREEN...

FIRST WE HAVE TO PUT ON THE SECOND COAT.

A COAT? DO I LOOK LIKE A BABY?!

NO, THE SECOND LAYER IS WHEN WE PAINT AGAIN...

THAT'S WHY I HAVE TWO CANS OF PAIN LEFT.

GREAT! OOH, YOU'RE THE NICEST SISTER IN THE WHOLE WIDE UNIVERSE!

???

I'LL GET EVERYTHING READY!

UH, HEY, MAUREEN, THAT SECOND COAT...

...IT'S FOR *MY* ROOM!

≠PFFF!⦓... YOU'RE THE WORSTEST IN THE WHOLE WIDE UNIVERSE!

CAZENOVE & WILLIAM

I LOVE IT! IT'S SUPER MEGA PRETTY. WE CRUSHED IT, GIRLS.

EVEN SO, MY PART OF THE WALL'S THE PRETTIEST, RIGHT?!

HEE-HEE!

AND NOW THE THREE OF US CAN PLAY A QUICK GAME OF CATCH. I'LL GO GET LOTS OF CUSHIONS.

NONONO. HOLD IT RIGHT THERE.

FIRST WE HAVE TO WASH THE BRUSHES.

WHY? IS THE PAINT DIRTY?

NO, BUT IF WE DON'T DO THAT, THE PAINT WILL DRY, THE BRISTLES WILL GET CAKED, AND WE'LL HAVE TO THROW THEM AWAY... DAD WON'T LIKE IT VERY MUCH.

HE'LL HAVE ANOTHER ANGRY OUTBREAK?!

AYAAA... WE NEED TO PUT THEM INTO THE WASHING MACHINE, QUICK!

LOOK, YOU DIP THEM IN WATER AND YOU RUB THE BRISTLES A LITTLE...

IT ISN'T HARD...

WOOOW! THE WATER GOT ALL BLUE. IT'S MAGIC!

PFF!... NOT AT ALL! IT'S THAT THE PAINT'S GETTING DILUTED.

I'M GOING TO FIND MORE BUCKETS, SO LOTS OF OTHER COLORS CAN BE GETTING DELUDED...

MWAH-HA-HA. MY SISTER'S REALLY TALENTED AT MISUNDERSTANDING EVERYTHING.

I'D SAY, INSTEAD, THAT SHE'S REALLY TALENTED AT MAKING YOU WASH THE PAINTBRUSHES FOR HER.

BOMBS AWAY!

KA-BOOM!

CAZENOVE & WILLIAM

WOW!

I LOVE IT TO PIECES! IT'S SWEET OF YOU TO GIVE ME A POSTER OF MY FAVORITE SERIES, MAUREEN.

WELL, SINCE I KNOW YOU LOVE IT AND YOU'RE LOOKING FOR PRETTY THINGS TO DECORATE YOUR NEW, ALL PRETTY ROOM WITH...

THANKS, SISTER. YOU'RE SO SWEET.

IS THIS WHERE YOU'D LIKE THE HOLE?

WHAAAT? WH-WHAT HOLE?

YOU'RE NUTS... WHERE'D YOU HEAR YOU SHOULD MAKE HOLES IN A WALL TO PUT UP A POSTER?!

THAT'S WHAT TAPE IS FOR!

YOU ALWAYS HAVE TO SPOIL EVERYTHING.

IF YOU'RE GOING TO BE LIKE THAT, I'M TAKING BACK MY PRESENT. NAH!

SHWIPP

SPTZZ

IT STILL WAS NICE OF HER TO OFFER YOU THAT POSTER...

÷PFFF!÷... YOU CAN TALK.

I KNOW THAT LITTLE MISS AND SHE ISN'T INTERESTED IN DECORATING...

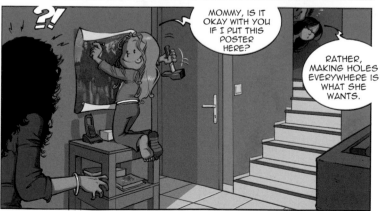

?!

MOMMY, IS IT OKAY WITH YOU IF I PUT THIS POSTER HERE?

RATHER, MAKING HOLES EVERYWHERE IS WHAT SHE WANTS.

21

CAZENOVE & WILLIAM

CAZENOVE & WILLIAM

AWWW... THAT'S SO CUTE!

WHAT'S SO CUTE, SAMMIE?

YOUR SISTER...

SHE'S ARRANGING ALL HER PLASTIC ANIMALS AND FIGURES... SHE'S SETTING UP A GIANT PETTING ZOO...

QUICK! QUIIIICK! GET DOWN, HURRY!

HUH?

WHAT'S GOING ON, WENDY? YOUR SISTER'S PLAYING CALMLY FOR ONCE...

GET DOWN, I'M TELLING YOU!

WOW... IT'S COMING! IT'S HERE! ≥TREMBLE!≤

CHATTER CHATTER

THERE! TOOORNAAADO... WOOOOUH...

WITH MAUREEN, THERE ARE NO CALM GAMES.

CAZENOVE & WILLIAM

AH... THAT'S IT? THE TORNADO'S BLOWN OVER?!

MPFRGZZMPR...

GOT TO NAP... ⇉MPFFF!⇇...

?!?!

MMMFFF...

SNOOONRZZzzz...

20 MINUTES LATER...

⇉YAWN!⇇....

WOOOOOW... I SLEPT SOOO WELL... ⇉MOOAH!⇇...

YEEEHAAAAW... FULL SPEED AHEAD!

ZZOOOOUM...

I'M TELLING YOU, SAMMIE...

MY SISTER IS TOTALLY ADORABLE WHEN SHE'S TIRED...

BUT YOU CAN'T BELIEVE HOW MUCH WORK IT IS TO WEAR HER OUT.

BALL... BALL...

I GOT IT! I GOT IT!

TO ME! TO ME!

CAZENOVE & WILLIAM

OKAY! OKAY! OKAY! IF YOU INSIST, I'LL SHOW YOU, BUT YOU MAY BE TOTALLY DISGUSTED.

HA. NO WORRIES.

WELL, IT'S YOUR CALL, MAUREEN.

YES, YES, IT'S MY CALL.

SO GREAT.

SO GREAT.

SO GREAT.

SO GR--

??? ?

OKAY, SO, ARE YOU COMING OR NOT?

IT'S HERE.

BUT, BUT, THAT'S, BUT--

YES, IT'S HERE, IN YOUR ROOM, STASHED BEHIND YOUR OLD BABY BOOKS YOU DON'T READ ANY LONGER.

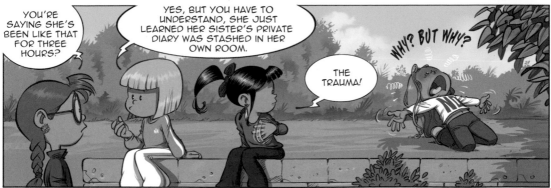

YOU'RE SAYING SHE'S BEEN LIKE THAT FOR THREE HOURS?

YES, BUT YOU HAVE TO UNDERSTAND, SHE JUST LEARNED HER SISTER'S PRIVATE DIARY WAS STASHED IN HER OWN ROOM.

THE TRAUMA!

WHY? BUT WHY?

25

CAZENOVE & WILLIAM

WENDY... DID YOU SEE? THERE'S A BABY BIRDLING ON THE GROUND.

OH, THE POOR THING... IT MUST HAVE FALLEN OUT OF MY TREE.

TWEET!

YES, AND SINCE I'M THE ONE WHO FOUND IT, IT'S MINE!

OF COURSE.

AND YOU CAN'T KEEP ME FROM CLIMBING YOUR TREE TO PUT IT BACK IN ITS NEST, WHICH IS ALSO MINE.

YES, YES.

NO PROBLEM, SISTER.

TWEET!

THE TREE IS MINE. THE NEST IS YOURS. I'M ALL GOOD WITH THAT.

THAT'S AWESOME, YOU KNOW!

TWEET!

SO, YOU'LL PAY ME RENT FOR LEASING MY BRANCH SO YOU CAN HAVE YOUR NEST THERE.

WHAT?!

TWEET!

THAT'LL BE TWELVE LOLLIPOPS...

...FOOT MASSAGES EVERY EVENING...

AND I GET TO CHOOSE ALL THE TV SHOWS.

TWEET!

EXCUSE ME, SIR...

...DO YOU KNOW HOW MUCH RENTING THIS TREE COSTS?

CAZENOVE & WILLIAM

WENDY TAKES CARE OF HER TREE LIKE A BIG SISTER ALL YEAR LONG...

SHE WATERS IT VERY EARLY WHEN IT'S TOO HOT.

DRINK UP!

YOU WERE THIRSTY, YEAH?

SHE TALKS TO IT SO IT DOESN'T GET LONELY.

AND THEN, MASON PLACED HIS SOFT LIPS ON MY HAND...

INSTANT MAGIC.

SHE GIVES IT THE BEST FERTILIZER SO IT CAN GET EVEN MORE BEAUTIFUL...

A TONIC FOR BEAUTIFUL LEAVES.

SHE DOES EVERYTHING SHE CAN TO KEEP IT FROM CATCHING COLD WHEN IT'S FREEZING...

THERE YOU GO... AND I'LL GO FIND YOU ANOTHER QUILT.

AND SINCE SHE TAKES GOOD CARE OF IT AND ALL, WELL, IT MAKES GREAT SHADE IN THE SUMMER.

THAT'S THE CATCH, IN MY OPINION, MAUREEN.

YOU DIDN'T TAKE GOOD ENOUGH CARE OF YOUR UMBRELLA LAST YEAR.

CAZENOVE & WILLIAM

CAZENOVE & WILLIAM

I'M FED UP! FED UP!

YOU'RE NOT MY SISTER ANYMORE!

STOP YOUR BELLYACHING!

THAT'LL TEACH YOU TO RUMMAGE THROUGH MY ROOM.

I DIDN'T RUMMAGE THROUGH ANYTHING AND BESIDES, STOP SPITTING ON MY NOSE!

OH, NO, WENDY AND MAUREEN ARE FIGHTING AGAIN.

YUP, AND THEY AREN'T PRETENDING, EITHER.

≈WHEW!!≈

THAT'S A NOSE? HA HA! IT LOOKS MORE LIKE A ROTTEN EGG...

I'LL BE BACK LATER. I HATE IT WHEN THEY BICKER LIKE THAT.

SAY THAT AGAIN, YOU BIG LUMP...

ROTTEN EGG, ROTTEN EGG...

HEY THERE, GIRLS, WHERE'RE YOU GOING?

...ROTTEN EGG, ROTTEN EGG...

STOP IT ALREADY, YOU UGLY, PUGLY PARROT.

WENDY?

BUT, BUT, WHAT... YOU'RE NOT HOME? SO WHO'S YOUR SISTER FIGHTING WITH, THEN?

GET OUT OF MY ROOM RIGHT NOW!

KRRRR₂...

WELL, WITH ME, REALLY...

MAUREEN RECORDS ALL OUR FIGHTS AND REPLAYS THE MIX SHE'S MADE OF HER FAVORITES.

WHEN YOU OPEN YOUR MOUTH, FLIES ZOOM OUT!

AND YOUR FEET STINK!

29

CAZENOVE & WILLIAM

In the depths of the earth lives a demon that feeds on tree energy...

SLURP!

BUT IF ONE OF THE TREES GETS HURT, THEN THE DEMON AWAKENS...

BOM BOM BOM

BOBO?

....AND RISES TO THE SURFACE TO DEMOLISH EVERYTHING...

BWAAAAK...

IT'S GINGKO!

AND IT SEEMS LIKE HE'S IN A BAD MOOD!

GRAB HIS ARMS, MAUREEN!

WHA... WHAT... DO... YOU... THINK... I'M AL-READY...

...DOING... OOOOH... SPINNING

HE'S HEAVY!

THERE WE GO, HE'S CALMING DOWN.

OKAY, GRINGKO, I'LL TELL FOLKS NOT TO BOTHER YOU.

GO TO SLEEP, BIG GUY.

GRING...

BUT GINGKO, THE TERRIFYING DEMON, IS READY TO WAKE UP AGAIN AT THE SLIGHTEST BLOW TO A TREE...

ALL THAT SO YOUR SISTER WON'T BOUNCE HER BALL AGAINST YOUR TREE ANYMORE?

IT WORKS! LOOK, SHE WON'T EVEN LET THE BIRDS GET CLOSE.

SO GOOD!

HA! HA! HA!

GET GOING! GO LOOK ELSEWHERE.

SHOO!

CAZENOVE & WILLIAM

CAZENOVE & WILLIAM

CAZENOVE & WILLIAM

KNOCK
KNOCK
KNOCK

?!

EEEPPP?!

HUG!

YOU WANT ME TO LEND YOU SOMETHING?!

NO, JUST A HUG.

AH, YESSS... SNACK TIME'S SOON...

AND YOU WANT ME TO MAKE YOU NULTELA CREPES WITH A BIG CHEESE BANANA SMOOTHIE.

NOPE. A HUG. THAT'S ALL.

OKAY, WELL, THEN, A HUG!

I LOVE YOU SOOOO MUCH!

THANKS, WENDY!

THE PEST'S SUCH A SWEETIE.

IT'S CRAZY HOW A HUG PEPS YOU UP!

IF YOU INSIST, YOU COULD STILL LEND ME YOUR TABLET AND MAKE ME SOME CREPES AND A SMOOTHIE.

YOU'RE THE BEST!

THANKS, SIS!

I'M AT THE END OF MY ROPE.

CAZENOVE & WILLIAM

AND THERE, RIGHT BEHIND THE LAUNDRY ROOM, IS...

...MY DADDY'S STUDIO. THAT'S WHERE HE DRAWS, WHERE HE MAKES HIS COMIC BOOKS, AND ALL THAT...

WOW! CAN WE VISIT IT?!

WELL, ACTUALLY, I'M NOT ALLOWED TO STEP FOOT IN THERE.

ESPECIALLY SINCE I KNOCKED OVER ALL THE INDIA INK ON HIS PAGES AND MADE ORIGAMI WITH THEM.

OOOH... SO LAME! YOU CAN'T GO IN THERE AT ALL?!

≥PFFF≤...HA HA... I'VE BEEN IN THERE LOTS OF TIMES, WHATCHA THINK?

THEY DON'T CALL ME "MASTER KEY MAUREEN," FOR NOTHING.

HEE-HEE-HEE!

KREE KREE KREE KREE KREE

AND PRESTO! THERE YOU GO! IT'S OPEN.

GREAT! GREAT! GREAT!

OKAY, WELL, SO SHALL WE GO IN?!

COME ON, ARE WE GOING TO ROOT AROUND?!

YES, YES, WE'RE GOING IN, WE'RE GOING IN...

ARE YOU GOING TO MAKE US KEEP WAITING?

NOW THAT YOU'VE GOT OUR MOUTHS WATERING...

SOOOO... WHEN'RE WE GOING IN?

AS SOON AS MY FATHER GETS BACK...

IT'S NO FUN TO GO WHERE YOU'RE NOT ALLOWED WHEN THERE'S NO ONE HOME TO CATCH YOU.

CAZENOVE & WILLIAM

WHEN SHE WAS A SMURFETTE, MAUREEN COULDN'T LIE... LIKE ALL BABIES, YOU KNOW.

SO, IS MOM'S PUREE GOOD?

NOM NOM NOM

HEY!

≶POUAH!≶ PUREE NO GOOD!

≶POUAH!≶ YOUR DRAWING'S NO GOOD, DADA.

≶POUAH!≶

WENDY SMELLS NO GOOD!

BAMBOO MAG

THEN SHE GREW AND LEARNED HOW TO LIE...

YUM... YOUR MINT ZUCCHINI JUICE IS SCRUMPTIOUS, MOMMY.

≶POUAH!≶

YOU WANT TO TASTE, WENDY?

UMM, THANKS, BUT I HAVE TO GO...

MASE AND SAMMIE ARE WAITING FOR ME AT THE MOVIE THEATRE.

WOW! YOUR NEW JACKET LOOKS SOOO GOOD ON YOU, WENDY!

YOU'RE LOOKING SHARP!

AS A RESULT, I ALWAYS DOUBT WHATEVER SHE SAYS NOW.

CAZENOVE & WILLIAM

HA HA. STAR POSE.

RHEE-ANNA, THAT'S ME!

CLICKA CLICKA CLICKA

THE BEST, YOU KNOW.

AND THERE YOU GO.

ALREADY? WOW, THAT'S EXTRA QUICK.

YUUP. THAT'S A CELL PHONE, SISTER.

WOW!

YOU'VE GOT A HIGH-TECH APP ON IT THAT ALSO TAKES PICTURES.

I'M SOOO PRETTY IN NIGH-TECH.

IT ALSO HAS A PHONE, TV, COMPASS, GPS, CALCULATOR, ALARM...

A TV, TOO? WOW!

YES, ALSO A CALENDAR, AND A--

OOPS... SPEAKING OF CALENDARS... I'VE GOT TO DASH OFF AND GET READY, OR ELSE I'LL KEEP SAMMIE WAITING.

AND SAMMIE HATES WAITING...

LATER, MAUREEN.

HOP HOP HOP

ZWIPP

⇒PFFF.⇐ I KNEW IT! WENDY WAS LYING TO IMPRESS ME. THERE'S NO CAMERA OR CAMERA LENS INSIDE IT.

I TOLD YOU SO. IT WOULDN'T FIT.

AND WHERE'S THE TV?

CAZENOVE & WILLIAM

I DON'T KNOW HOW YOU DO THAT, MAUREEN...

IT ISN'T REALLY HARD. I KEEP SHOWING YOU.

DRIVING ME NUTS... THE PAPER'S TOTALLY LAME, TOO.

FOR THE THIRD TIME, YOU FOLD THE PAPER IN HALF, AND THEN YOU FOLD EACH HALF BY BRINGING THE TIP TO THE MIDDLE.

THERE, LIKE THAT, YOU SEE?

CRUNG!

YOU FOLD IT AGAIN HERE. FOLD THE SIDES AGAIN. TURN THEM UP TO MAKE THE FINS...

AND YOU TUCK IN THE CORNER THAT POKES OUT.

THERE! A NICE JET PLANE!

THIS TIME I FEEL LIKE I'M GOING TO DO IT.

WOOOOSH!

OKAY THE FOLDINGING. JUST THE WAY IT SHOULD BE.

...THERE! I FOLD--:GNNNAAA...!⸮

SONG

WHAT ARE YOU DOING, BRATS?

ORIGAMI, WENDY!

AND HERE'S A NICE PET AIRPLANE.

...

WROOOOOMM!

MWAH-HA-HA... FUNNY-LOOKING PLANE, HA HA HA, I LOVE IT!

HA HA HA HA HA HA

HEHEE HEE

AT LEAST YOU'VE MADE SOME PROGRESS. YOU MANAGED TO FOLD YOUR SISTER OVER.

CAZENOVE & WILLIAM

...YOUR BROTHER'S LEAVING THE PICTURE, THEN IT'LL BE YOUR SISTER'S TURN, AND UNLESS YOU FIX THIS MESS, YOU'LL FOLLOW...

...AH, THAT'S NO GOOD! NO, IT STARTS AT THE TOP, I'M TELLING YOU.

TLUNK

TSOING

STONK

YAY!

LOOK, WENDY, LULU! MY NAIRPLANE IS SOOO PRETTY!

PLUS, IT'S SUPER HARD TO MAKE.

I'M GOING TO SHOW IT TO EVERYYYBODY...

MOMMY! DAAAADDY!

YOU KNOW WHAT, LULU? LET'S SHOW MAUREEN OUR ORIGAMI LATER.

DEFINITELY. OTHERWISE, SHE'LL BE DEPRESSED THE WHOLE DAY.

HEE-HEE!

38

CAZENOVE & WILLIAM

CLIKA

BLEH!... IT'S BLURRY.

CLIKA

YOU CAN DO IT, RIGHT?

MUCH BETTER.

CLIKA

DO YOU WANT ME TO CALL 911?

JUST A SEC, IT ISN'T EASY!

I NEED CONCENTRA-TIONISM...

SO, SHHH!

CLIKA CLIKA

WHATEVS!

BAH, *PFFF!*... IT'S EVEN BLURRIER.

HOW DO YOU DO IT?

GIVE ME THAT. I'M GOING TO TAKE THE PICTURE MYSELF.

NOOOO... I'LL DO IT. I'LL DO IT.

YOU'RE UNTALENTED. YOU'RE UNTALENTED. THAT'S ALL.

YEEAHHH. WELL, IT ISN'T MY FAULT! YOUR TREE KEEPS MOVING! SO THERE!

SHE REALLY BELIEVES WHAT SHE'S SAYING, WENDY...

HA HA HA!

YOU'RE BARKING UP THE WRONG TREE, GIRL.

CAZENOVE & WILLIAM

CRUNCH

CRUNCH
CRUNCH
CRUNCH

MUNCH
MUNCH

PFFT MUAHAH HA HA
HA HA HA
HA HA
HA

EEEEEK!

GOOD GOING, WENDY! VERY
SMART TO TELL JOKES WHILE
WE'RE EATING.

SORRY... IT
JUST SLIPPED
OUT.

40

CAZENOVE & WILLIAM

WAIT, WENDY. I'LL DO IT.

UHH... YES.

IF YOU WANT, SAMMIE. BUT IT'S THE KIND OF RIDDLE THAT HAS TO BE READ VERY, VERY QUICKLY.

NO WORRIES, I'VE GOT IT ALL UNDER CONTROL.

MAAAUREEEN... WE'VE GOT A TREASURE HUNT FOR--

--YOU.

I LOVE TREASURE HUNTS SOOOO MUCH!

WHAT'S THE RIDDLE?

PANT PANT

WHAT IS IT?

LISTEN CAREFULLY.

I WON'T REPEAT IT.

SO, IN THE GARDEN...

UNDER THE WATERING CAN, YOU'LL FIND THE FIRST CLUE.

...DECIPHERING IT NOW IS UP TO YOU...

AND TO DO THAT, FIRST SHOW YOUR WIT AND--

FORGET IT, SAMMIE.

YOU NEEDED TO READ IT MUCH, AND I MEAN MUCH, MORE QUICKLY.

I'M GOING TO FIND THE CLUE...

I'M GOING TO FIND IT...

I'M GOING TO FIND IT...

I'M GOING TO FIND THE CLUE...

?!

CAZENOVE & WILLIAM

...A GREAT DAD. TRALALALA TRALALALA TRALALALA TRALALALA... HE'S REALLY...

HE'S REALLY...
HE'S REALLY...
HE'S REALLY...

THAT WAS FOR DAD'S BIRTHDAY.

I'M SIIIIICK WITH LOVE FOR YOU, MOMMY. I'M SIIICK WITH LOVE FOR YOUUUUU... IT'S YOUR BIRTHDAY, YOU SEE AND WITHOUT YOU, I'M SIIIICKKK...

MOM'S...

THEIR ANNIVERSARY...

AAAAGAAADOODOODOO. YOU'RE THE COOLEST COUPLE, AGADOODOODOO. YOU'RE THE HANDSOMEST COUPLE...

BRAVO! AMAZING!
WHAT TALENT! SUPER!
THANK YOU!
CLAP CLAP CLAP
CLAP CLAP CLAP

PHEW! ... LUCKY THEY ONLY CELEBRATE OUR BIRTHDAYS AND ANNIVERSARY.

YES, IT'S ADORABLE. BUT TWO HOURS OF "ENTERTAINMENT" EACH TIME IS...

...EXHAUSTING.

AH. THE CHOCOLATE TART IS READY.

YOU'RE REALLY, YOU'RE REALLY, THE CHOCOLATE TART WORLD CHAMP, LALALALA LA LA LA LA LALALALA LALEEERE... YOU'RE REALLY...

SIGH.

CAZENOVE & WILLIAM

HEEEY, MAUREEN... WHY'D YOU SEND ME A PAPER AIRPLANE WITH "ON" WRITTEN ON IT?

WAIT, THERE'RE LOTS MORE OF THEM.

SAID?

DEAR?

???

BU?

WELL, WHAT'S THIS GOBBLEDY-GOOK?

AH, NO! YOU HAVE TO FIGURE OUT THE CODED MESSAGE. IF NOT, IT'S CHEATING.

HEY THERE, BRAT. DO YOU REALLY THINK I HAVE NOTHING BETTER TO DO THAN PLAY AROUND WITH A MYSTERY MESSAGE?

I KNOW WHAT THE MESSAGE SAYS!

IT MEANS, "MASON CALLED AND HE SAID THAT HE AND HIS BUDDIES WERE COMING TO GET YOU IN TWENTY MINUTES."

YUUPPP... YAAAAYYY, MASON. YOU FIGURED IT OUT!

CAZENOVE & WILLIAM

HEY! SHRIMP...

COME HERE.

I KNOW I FORBADE YOU TO TOUCH ANYTHING IN MY ROOM...

...TO RUMMAGE AROUND, JUMP ON MY BED, AND SCREAM...

WELL, YES, AND YOU'VE SEEN HOW DULL IT IS AS A RESULT.

YUPPP! YOU WERE RIGHT, SIS.

I'M GOING TO CHANGE ALL THAT.

SO, I'LL BE ABLE TO DO EVERYTHING THAT I USED TO DO IN YOUR ROOM AGAIN?

DID IT WORK?

⇒PFF!⇐... I DON'T GET IT... NOW SHE'S FORBIDDEN ME FROM EVEN GOING IN.

TOO LAME!

CAZENOVE & WILLIAM

AAAAAAMMM... PFFFFF...

FLEB
FLEB
FLEB
FLEB

GRUMPF!

AAAAAAAA...

PFFFFE.. PFFFE.. PFFFE..

PFFFFFFFFFFFFFFFFFFFFFFFFFFFFFF...

...FFF CHOMP

AMPFFFF...

I CANNNN'T DOOOOO IT... I'M SO BAAAAD AT INFLATIONING BALLOOOOONS...

BWAAAA...

SOME FRESH AIR?!

WATCH.

FFF FFF FFFFF

THE TOUGHEST PART IS TYING THE KNOT.

PRESTO, BINGO, THERE YOU GO. WHAT'RE YOU GOING TO DO WITH YOUR BALL--

POP

BURST IT!

I JUST ADORE THAT SOUND.

GAAAH!

CAZENOVE & WILLIAM

WHAT? ARE YOU SERIOUS?!

YOU, YOU, YOU AREN'T GOING TO DO THAT, RIGHT?

...TEAR DOWN MY TREE, THE ONE THAT'S MINE, JUST TO BE ABLE TO PUT IN A NEW TERRACE?!

BUT, THAT'S BARBARIC!

STILL, IT'S NOT JUST A TREE...

IT'S A LIVING BEING YOU PLANTED AFTER I WAS BORN.

THAT'S A BIG DEAL... CAN YOU IMAGINE ALL THE MEMORIES WE SHARE?!

IT'S THE BROTHER I NEVER HAD...

MY OTHER SELF. THE MIRROR OF MY LIFE. ALL THAT.

BESIDES, YOU COULD JUST AS WELL PUT THE TERRACE AROUND IT COULDN'T YOU?

ISN'T THAT POSSIBLE?!

OKAY, OKAY, WENDY, YOU WIN!

WE WON'T TOUCH A LEAF ON YOUR TREE... IT WILL HAVE ITS OWN SPOT IN THE NEW TERRACE AND THAT WILL BE VERY NICE.

HEY... YOU ALSO NEED TO LEAVE A SPOT FOR ME!

BUT... YOU DON'T HAVE A TREE IN THE GARDEN, MAUREEN.

ANYWAY...

AND THAT'S THE EXACT SPOT WHERE I DROPPED MY BOTTLE THE FIRST TIME WHEN I WAS A BABY...

WELL... IT WOULD'VE BEEN A PITY TO HAVE COVERED THAT UP, TOO.

CAZENOVE & WILLIAM

HA-HA!... EXCELLENT. I LOVE IT WHEN THEY JUMP OUT OF THE PLANE.

THEY NEVER GET HURT. THEY'RE INDESTROYABLE.

VROOOOO...

WOULDN'T YOU THINK IT WAS CRAZY IF WE WERE CARTOON HEROINES?

LIKE KIM POSSIBLE, TOTALLY SPIES, AND DORA?

THAT WOULD BE SO GREAT.

AND WE'D HAVE TONS OF ADVENTURES WITH ALL OUR FRIENDS... THERE'D BE LULU, NAT, SAMMIE, AND YOUR MASON GLUESTICK.

WE'D BE ABLE TO HAVE MEGA-FIGHTS IN OUR ROOMS, WITH OUR PILLOWS, AND EVEN DADDY AND MOMMY SUPERVISORINGS, WOOOW...

GRUMBLYOUTNOOO

WE'D PUNCH ZOMBIES IN THE FACE.

BAFF

WE'D CAPTURE THE NEIGHBOR'S GARDEN GNOME THAT DOES VOODOO MAGIC...

FULL SPEED AHEAD...

WE'D GET TO RACE CLIMBERING ALONG ON "SCOOTERJUMPS!"

AND EVERYONE'D SEE WE'RE THE MOST FANTASTIC SISTERS IN THE UNIVERSE!

WE'D CALL IT "THE SISTERS!"

UH, NO, NOT AT ALL. WE SHOULD CALL IT "THE ADVENTURES OF MAUREEN...."

OTHERWISE, NOBODY WOULD WANT TO WATCH IT!

CAZENOVE & WILLIAM

RAH LA LA... I LOVE GOING BACK TO THE HOUSE WE GREW UP IN.

DID YOU SEE?! OUR PARENTS KEPT OUR TOYS.

DID YOU SEE?! IT'S GREAT OUR PARENTS KEPT OUR TOYS!

WHAT'S GREAT TO SEE IS THAT YOU STILL REPEAT EVERYTHING OVER AND OVER.

HUH? WHAT... WHAT ARE YOU TALKING ABOUT?

WELL, YES. LOOK, YOU'VE ALWAYS DONE THAT.

YOU REPEAT THINGS ALL THE TIME.

I WANT THE REMOTE! I WANT THE REMOTE!

POOH!

I GET THE FIRST CREPE. I GET THE FIRST CREPE.

WENDY HIT ME. WENDY HIT ME.

BUT IT'S TRUE. AND THAT'S ONE YOU USED TO SAY AT LEAST TEN TIMES A DAY.

HA! HA! HA!

I KNOW SOMEONE ELSE WHO WAS A LOT WORSE THAN ME.

AH, NO. I DON'T THINK SO.

YOU'VE GOT A SHORT MEMORY.

WELL?

GET DOWN! GET DOWN FROM MY TREE RIGHT NOW!

SEE?! YOU'VE BEEN REPEATING THAT OVER AND OVER FOR YEARS.

48

CAZENOVE & WILLIAM

HOW MANY SLEEPS IS IT UNTIL "TALOUINE"?

AT FIRST, IT WASN'T EASY TO GET MY SISTER TO UNDERSTAND THE CONCEPT OF HALLOWEEN...

NO, *MAUREEN*, IT'S CALLED "HAL-LO-WEEN."

TALOUINE IS A RARE BIRD.

WHY DO I HAVE TO DRESS LIKE A NASTY WITCH?

AM I BEING PUNISHED?

I DIDN'T DO ANYTHING!

COSTUMES

THESE "PAJUMPKINS" GROW FAST. DO WE HAVE TO EAT THEM ALL?

MUARF!

BUT I'M TELLING YOU THAT THE WOMAN GIVES US CANDY...

NOT THE OPPOSITE.

MINE, ALL MINE!

AND FINALLY... ONE DAY...

OH, YEAH!

I GET IT ALL!

THE HARDEST THING WAS TO GET HER TO UNDERSTAND THAT HALLOWEEN DOESN'T LAST THE WHOLE YEAR.

SO... WHO WANTS TO GO GET CANDY FROM THE NEIGHBORS WITH ME?

BIG, BIG SIGHS!

COME ON...LET'S ALL GO!

49

CAZENOVE & WILLIAM

MY NAME'S ARROW!

THE FASTEST ARROW IN THE UNIVERSE.

I LOVE IT! IT FITS YOU PERFECTLY.

YOU'RE INDESTROYINGABLE, MAUR--

--EEN.

ZZZZZ ZZZZZZZZ ZZZOOMM

LOOMM

CHOP SBAF WiiiZZ

OH, OUCHIEE!

BOINK

YEAH, WELL. IT DOESN'T WORK. NO MORE OF THAT... ÷ARGH!÷...

YOU STILL HAVE INVISIBLE GIRL'S COSTUME TO TRY.

WE'LL MANAGE TO STEAL YOUR SISTER'S DIARY EVENTUALLY.

CAZENOVE & WILLIAM

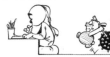

YEEHAAAAAAW!

K8!

HAH!

SWIIIP

SBOK

MISSED! HEH HEH!

B12!

FAILED!

SSSWWW

GET YOUR EYES CHECKED! HEE-HEE!

D8!

WRONG!

H2! A9! V5! F7!

YOU'RE BLIND!

LOSER!

P4! J11!

SBONF

M6! F4! W9!

K4!

CHTONF
CHTONF
CHTONF
CHTONF

OKAY... OKAY... SAN-SANK! MMPH...

RATTLESHIP WITH THE SISTERS IS HEAVY DUTY!

DO YOU WANT TO PLAY A ROUND?

UHHH... NO, NO!

NO WAY!

PHOO...

CAZENOVE & WILLIAM

AY YAI YAI! HER FAVORITE DRESS... YOUR SISTER WILL TOTALLY KILL YOU!

MMM... UNLESS I CAN SEW IT BACK UP.

WHY ARE YOU LOOKING IN YOUR FATHER'S STUDIO?

THERE'S EVERYTHING YOU NEED HERE: STAPLES, SUPERGLUX, AND EVEN THUMBTACKS.

RUSTLE RATTLE

MY MOTHER DOES IT WITH NEEDLE AND THREAD.

WELL, YEAH, BUT I'M NOT ALLOWED TO TOUCH ANY NEEDLES, OR ANYTHING THAT PRICKS OR CUTS.

AH! I FOUND IT!

YOU KNOW, IF I GLUE SOME CARDBOARD THERE WHERE IT'S TORN AND COLOR IT THE SAME COLOR AS THE DRESS WITH A FELT-TIP PEN...

...THEN I ATTACH IT WITH PAPERCLIPS OR BIG RUBBERY BANDOS.

PLUS, IT'S NOT MY FAULT. I JUST WANTED TO PLAY PRINCESS DAENERYS AND HER MINI-ME.

I BARELY PULLED ON IT WHEN I CLIMBED ON MY DRAGONETTE...

...AND IT GOT ALL TORN.

BUT WENDY'S DRESS IS GARBAGE.

OKAY! THEY LOOK ALIKE BUT MINE IS TOTALLY STRONGER!

THEY'RE EXACTLY IDENTICAL, MAUREEN!

OH, JEEPERS! YOU'RE SO RIGHT, ALANIS...

HEE HEE HEE!

THANKS, COUSIN!

UHHHH... SOMEONE OWES ME AN EXPLANATION HERE...

??

LA

W

CAZENOVE & WILLIAM

IT ISN'T FAR, MAUREEN.

THERE! ON THE COUCH!

WAH-HOO!

I'VE GOT IT!

PRESTO! INTO DA BOX!

YESSSS! PLUS, IT'S A MEGA RARE ONE.

WHAT'S ALL THE FUSS?

WE'RE HUNTING POKÉMON, MOMMY.

THEY'RE ALL OVER!

IT'S AN APP ON MY PHONE, A GAME.

IT'S SO AWESOME!

DO YOU WANT TO HUNT WITH US, TOO?!

ALL THE POKÉMON AROUND SHOW UP ON YOUR SCREEN. YOU JUST HAVE TO GRAB THEM, HEH-HEH...

AHH, OKAY. I SEE... NICE!

THEN YOU SHOULD LIKE THIS OTHER APPLICATION.

...I'LL INSTALL IT, PRESTO! AND THERE.

ALL YOUR THINGS LYING AROUND THAT YOU SHOULD PUT AWAY SHOW UP ON THE SCREEN.

YOU JUST HAVE TO GRAB THEM.

HEH-HEH...

53

CAZENOVE & WILLIAM

WENDY, WENDY, WENDY...

WILL YOU PLAY SUBITOS KANGAROO WITH ME NOW, HUH? WILL YOU PLAY, WILL YOU?!

...

YES! I GOT A DOUBLE SIX. I'M FINISHING MY THIRD TRIP AROUND THE PARK.

OOOH, NO... IT'S NOT FAIR.

AND I'LL TAKE YOUR KOALA CARD!

HEE HEE

WHAT? I DISAGREE. YOU ALREADY GOT LOTS OF KOALA CARDS.

YOU'RE NOTHING BUT A CHEATER. IT'S MY GAME AND I SHOULD GET TO WIN!

OH, HEY! THE DESERT DINGO HAD BETTER CALM HERSELF DOWN!

I'LL CALM DOWN IF I WANT TO!

ANYWAY, YOU NEVER UNDERSTAND MY RULES!

GROOAR!

OUCH!

MYEAH, NEVER MIND.

PHEW!...

EVEN I DON'T WANT TO PLAY WITH ME.

CAZENOVE & WILLIAM

NO, SERIOUSLY, WHAT DO YOU THINK OF THE NEW KID?

AH, NOELLE... WELL...

HER PROFILE PICTURES ROCK.

SHE'S PRETTY COOL.

SBLAM

YOO-HOO IN THERE!

WHAT DO YOU WANT, MAUREEN?

HOW'S IT GOING, GIRLS? I'D SAY YOU'RE BORED.

I BET YOU'VE MISSED ME SO MUCH?!

HA! HA!

BOING

BOING

HMMM... SAMMIE, YOU'RE MY FAV! ⇒KISS, KISS, KISS...⇐

SMACK, SMACK, SMACK

COME ON, SHALL WE PLAY SUBITOS KANGAROO?!

AND AFTERWARDS, CLOBBER EACH OTHER WITH PILLOWS...

...WE'LL RACE AND DRINK COCOLA THROUGH OUR NOSES WHILE––

GUK?!

STOP!

ENOUGH, BRAT! YOU'RE WEARING US OUT ALREADY!

GO PLAY WITH YOUR PALS.

WELL, YES, BUT...

...I ALREADY WORE THEM OUT JUST NOW.

CAZENOVE & WILLIAM

Panel 1:
IN THE EVENING, DAD, MOM, AND I ARE VERY CAREFUL ABOUT EVERYTHING WE DO...

ANOTHER ADVANTAGE OF THIS HIGH POSITION IS THAT THE BATS CAN AVOID GETTING EATEN BY FOUR-FOOTED PREDATORS...

Panel 2:
WE AVOID ANYTHING THAT COULD GET MAUREEN EXCITED... BECAUSE IF SHE GETS EXCITED...

THAT LIVE AND HUNT ON THE GROUND...

Panel 3:
...SHE STAYS LIKE THAT FOR HOURS!

YEAHHH! A "CAPE OF SWORDS" MOVIE, HA-HA!

I'M NAPOLEONA THE KNIGHT ON HER DRAGON!

YAHA!

EN GARDE, STEEDIE THE STURDY!

Panel 4:
AND THERE'S NO WAY THAT SHE'LL GO TO SLEEP UNTIL VERY LATE AT NIGHT...

...SHE'S A REAL WHIRL-WIND!

CAPTAIN PUDGE IS THROWING PUNCHES!

BUNK
BUNCH
BOK

Panel 5:
AS A RESULT, WE AVOID TALKING ABOUT GAMES OR SHOWS SHE LOVES...

YAAAAWWWW...

GETTING SLEEPY...

Panel 6:
WE PUT THE MOST SOPORIFIC SHOWS ON THE TV...

MMM... NICE, FLUFFY PILLOW...

ALL ROUND...

LIKE THE MOON...

Panel 7:
BUT IT ISN'T EASY...

YES! LIKE THE MOON!

Panel 8:
SUPER M BURSTS ONTO THE MOON...

...SHE'S GOING TO CRUSHIFY THE HORRIBLE STRATERRESTRIAL NINSECTS.

SHE'LL CLOBBER THEM!

IN SHORT, MAUREEN CAN GET HERSELF EXCITED FROM VERY LITTLE.

BOINK
BOINK
BOINK

56

GIRLS, THE TRIP OUT WEST WAS SO AWESOME!

THAT'S MONUMENT VALLEY. I WON'T TELL YOU ABOUT ALL THE MOVIES THEY SHOT AROUND THERE...

WAIT, I'VE GOT LOTS MORE PHOTOS. ONE DAY, WE TOOK A BUS SUPER EARLY IN THE MORNING...

TO SEE THE SUNRISE OVER THE GRAND CANYON...

WOW!

HOW LUCKY!

WE CROSSED THE NEVADA DESERT, ROUTE 66... LEGENDARY, DEATH VALLEY...

BOY, WAS IT HOT THERE.

THE ROCKIES REFLECTING IN THE LAKE WERE EPIC.

AND I WON'T EVEN TELL YOU ABOUT MT. RUSHMORE...

TOTALLY CRAZY!

AND DO YOU KNOW WHAT WE DID ONE DAY?

UUH...

NO, WHAT?

WE TOOK A BUS!

WOW!

HOW LUCKY!

CAZENOVE & WILLIAM

AS SOON AS WE TOOK OFF FOR HOME, MAUREEN DID HER MAUREEN THING...

SNOR ZZZ

THE DRIVER'S AN ACE, TO BE ABLE TO CROSS THROUGH ALL THOSE WIRES.

ALRIGHT, FIRST OFF, HE'S A PILOT AND WHAT WIRES ARE YOU TALKING ABOUT?

WELL, THE ONES HOLDING UP THE CLOUDS.

YOU'RE NOT GOING TO MAKE ME BELIEVE THEY FLOAT LIKE THAT IN THE SKY ALL BY THEMSELVES, UH-UH.

≥PFFF!≤... YOU WEAR ME OUT, MAUREEN.

OKAY, LISTEN. A CLOUD IS LIKE STEAM. IT'S LIGHTER THAN AIR, SO IT DOESN'T NEED A WIRE TO STAY SUSPENDED.

FOR REALS?

YUP!

AH, YES, WENDY, YOU'RE RIGHT. I CAN'T SEE A WIRE AT ALL.

JEEPERS, THAT'S CRAZY!

NOW THAT SHE'S EXPRESSED THAT OUTRAGEOUS THEORY TO ME, IT WILL BE CALM FOR A GOOD WHILE.

I MEAN, AS LONG AS THE STRING HOLDING THE PLANE IS STRONG.

CAZENOVE & WILLIAM

ARE YOU SURE IT WAS PUT AWAY UP HERE, WENDY?

YES, MAUREEN. I ALREADY SAW IT...

...IN A RED OR PINK SHOEBOX.

AH-HA! YEAH! HERE IT IS!

OPEN IT! OPEN IT! OPEN IT!

THERE'S A TON OF PAPERS. WHOA!

WHAT ARE THEY? TREASURE MAPS?!

OF COURSE NOT...

THESE ARE ALL OUR PARENTS' REPORT CARDS.

MOM GOT GREAT GRADES IN ALL HER SUBJECTS.

CAN YOU GET HIGHER THAN AN A+ IN MATH?

ARE DADDY'S THERE, TOO?

YES, AT THE BOTTOM OF THE BOX. LOOK.

NNLLAH HA HA HA HA HA HA HA WAAAHH HA HA HA HA HA HA HA HEE-HEE WAAAHH HEE-HEE HAHHAH PIP HI PIP!

MOM, CAN YOU HELP MAUREEN AND ME GET READY FOR OUR TESTS TOMORROW?

I CAN HELP, TOO!

UHH... NO, THAT'S OKAY, DADDY. WE'D RATHER DO WELL THIS TIME.

CAZENOVE & WILLIAM

GRUMBLL

GULP!

≒RAAH!≒... YOUR SISTER IS THE WORST OF ALL SISTERS, MAUREEN!

SLAM

YEAH! A REAL PILL BUG!

THE QUEEN OF PILL BUGS!

WHAT IF WE MADE UP A STORY ABOUT THE LIFE OF THE REALLY ABOMINABLE "WENDY-PILL-BUG?!"

OH, YEAH!

SUPER GREAT IDEA, LULU!

WE COULD TOTALLY MAKE IT INTO A COMICBOOK!

WITH LOTS OF VOLUMES.

I'VE GOT TONS OF THINGS TO INCLUDE ON TOP OF THAT.

I'LL MAKE THE DRAWINGS IN THE PANELS!

≒ARF!≒ NOT COOL! I WANTED TO DRAW, TOO.

HEEEYY, NO. I DRAW SUPER WELL, FOR STARTERS.

UNLESS...

LET ME GET THIS STRAIGHT, YOU WANT ME TO WRITE A STORY WHERE I SAY I'M A BIG PILL BUG?!

YES, BUT DON'T WORRY ABOUT THE DRAWINGS. WE'LL DO THEM.

CAZENOVE & WILLIAM

SO, WHAT FLAVOR DO YOU WANT, MAUREEN?

UHHH....

"YUM SLURP!"

MAYBE LEMON. BUT THAT'S ESPECIALLY BECAUSE IT'S MY FAVORITE COLOR OF ALL.

THE PROOF: I PUT UP A HUGE, ALL-YELLOW POSTER IN MY ROOM. MY FRIENDS WERE ALL SUPER JEALOUS. HEE-HEE. IT'S THE SUN, LOOKING LIKE A TWIN OF A TENNIS BALL.

I LOVE IT!

TOO PRETTY!

I PLAY TENNIS WITH WENDY OFTEN... I LOVE IT! I CAN HIT THE BALL LIKE A BRUTE.

POW

LAST TIME I WON EVERY GAME AND I DIDN'T EVEN HAVE TO CHEAT.

IMDABEST!

HELLLOOOO... IS THERE ANYONE THERE?

WE CAN'T TAKE ALL DAY HERE. WHAT DO YOU WANT?

PHEW!

TO BECOME THE BIGGEST TENNIS CHAMPION IN THE WHOLE WIDE WORLD.

?!

SHE WANTS LEMON!

??!?

CAZENOVE & WILLIAM

WILL YOU STOP GROUSING ALREADY, MAUREEN?

WE'RE DOING HALLOWEEN FOR YOU. YOU KNOW THAT?!

GRMGNB GRMGNN... MM.

I DIDN'T WANT TO WEAR A VAMPIIIIRE COSTUME...

IT'S TOO UGLY!

BUUUUAAAH... GROMPF!

WHAT DID YOU WANT TO DRESS UP AS?

WHATEVS.

BBB FROM "STAROUARZ." BUT WENDY NEVER WANTED THAT.

SHE MADE ME WEAR THIS TOTALLY ROTTEN COSTUME.

WHAT? IS THAT TRUE, WENDY? YOU FORCED HER?!

YES, SAMMIE. BUT THERE'S A REAL REASON...

...IT'S THE ONLY WAY FOR US TO BENEFIT EVEN A LITTLE FROM HALLOWEEN.

WITHOUT HER VAMPIRE TEETH, MAUREEN WOULD ALREADY HAVE SNARFED UP ALL THE CANDY.

IT ISN'T FAIR!

MM-MM

MEE-MEE

HA HA HA

CAZENOVE & WILLIAM

YOUR "NIGHT TALONS" ARE SUPER REALISTIC, WENDY.

YUP! MY FATHER MADE THE GLOVE.

AND YOUR COSTUME'S DEVILISHLY GOOD!

YOOHOO, MY SISTER'S SUPERBUDS...

?!

...YOU'RE DRESSED UP SOOO NICELY FOR YOUR HALLOWEEN PARTY.

YOU NEED YOUR STRENGTH TO GO COLLECTING CANDY TONIGHT...

SO, I MADE YOU A SUPER SNACK.

SOME NICE, SWEET HOT CHOCOLATE...

BUT BEFORE THAT, YOU'RE GOING TO LOVE MY SPECIALTY...

LEMON CARAMEL FONDANT CAKE!

WENDY, I TOOK ADVANTAGE OF YOUR BEING OUT HERE TO MAKE YOUR BED AND VACUUM YOUR ROOM.

AND I WASHED YOUR WINDOWS, TOO.

IF YOU'D LIKE MORE CAKE OR SOMETHING ELSE TO DRINK, YOU JUST CALL ME.

I WON'T BOTHER YOU ANYMORE... YOU'VE UNDOUBTEDLY GOT TONS OF THINGS TO SAY TO EACH OTHER.

ENJOY YOURSELVES!

WOW! DID YOU SEE THAT?!

=PHEW!=

HOLY COW!

=GULP!=

HER "ADORABLE SISTER" COSTUME FOR HALLOWEEN FREAKS ME OUT TOO MUCH.

TOTALLY!

63

CAZENOVE & WILLIAM

CAZENOVE & WILLIAM

THAT HIKE WAS GREAT! I'M WIPED OUT!

MY LEGS ARE SHOT.

SAME WITH ME! AND WE GOT BACK RIGHT ON THE DOT FOR..

..."VAMPIRE MOONLIGHT," SECOND SEASON... ⸨SQUEEEEE!⸩

MMM....

COULD YOU RECORD THE EPISODE ON THE TV HARD DRIVE, EMMA?

WELLL... DON'T YOU WANT TO WATCH IT WITH ME?

PHARRELL IS GOING TO MEET THE QUEEN OF THE IMMORTALS.

I'D REALLY LIKE TO, BUT YOU SEE...

...WHEN WE LEFT FOR OUR WALK, MY SISTER WAS RUNNING ERRANDS WITH MY PARENTS...

YUP, I KNOW. SO WHAT?

AND SINCE SHE WAS AT HER MODERN JAZZ CLASS THIS MORNING, I HAVEN'T SEEN HER EITHER.

SO, IS THAT SERIOUS?

WENDYYY...

...THE BEST SISTER IN MY WHOLE LIFE!

AH, WELL, SPEAK OF THE DEVIL...

I'VE GOT LOTS OF THINGAMA-JIGGERIES TO TELL YOU... YUPS...

...YOU KNOW THAT I GOT TO PICK THE TOMATOES.

AND AT THE CHECKOUT, I ALMOST GOT TWO BIKE TIRES...

...AND AFTER THAT, KNOW WHAT?...

AND WAIT, YOU KNOW WHAT?

OKAY, GOT IT! I'LL RECORD THE EPISODE AFTER THAT, TOO... HAHA!

BLA BLA BLA

CAZENOVE & WILLIAM

OKAY, MAUREEN, ARE YOU COMING OR WHAT?

WAIT, WENDY. COME LOOK AT THIS CRAZY THING.

WOOOW! I LOVE IT!

HA-HA! YOU'LL BE BEDIZZLDAZZLED!

BEDIZZLDAZZLED, ⋛PFFRRR.⋚

WHATEVS!

AND BING! IT WENT TO GREEN. WOW... WHEN I TOUCH MY NOSE, IT'S MAGIC!

YOU'RE THE BEST.

I CONTROL THE TRAFFIC LIGHT. I'M SUCH A MAGICIANERIAN.

BIG TIME! WE'LL CALL YOU MAUREEN POTTER.

IN THE CAR GOING TO SCHOOL WITH DADDY, TOO, I MADE ALL THE LIGHTS CHANGE... ASK HIM IF YOU DON'T BELIEVE ME.

YEAH, YEAH, ⋛MWARF!⋚ WE'LL NOTIFY THE PRESS...

AT LAST...

WHERE HAVE YOU BEEN?

I WAS WORRIED SICK. IT'S BEEN ALMOST AN HOUR SINCE YOU WENT TO BUY BREAD...

QUICK, MAUREEN, MAKE MOM CHANGE TO GREEN!

I'M TRYING, BUT IT ISN'T WORKING.

CAZENOVE & WILLIAM

YES! I GET THE POINT!

YOU LOST, MAUREEN.

IN YOUR DREAMS!

HEY, GIRLS...

TUNK

TUNK

YES, LOST! MAUREEN, TWO FORFEITS.

CHING CHING CHING

HEY, GIRLS...

MWAH-HA-HA! SUCH STYLE! ARF ARF...

...HEY, "WOODY-WENDY," WHERE'D YOU STABLE YOUR HORSE? IN THE LIVING ROOM?!

HIGH-HO, WENDY!

IT'S CUTE, WOODY!

NO WORRIES. IT'S JUST A COWBOY OUTFIT.

BESIDES, YOU SAY "COWGIRL" FOR GIRLS.

÷PFFF!÷... CHAOS, GIRRRL...

HA! HA!

SURELY YOU KNOW THAT COWBOYS WERE BOYS WHO COWHERDS?!

THAT MEANS THEY WATCHED OVER THE COWS IN THE FIELDS? ÷MWARF!÷...

EXACTLY, MAUREEN!

SO WHY'RE YOU DRESSED LIKE THAT?

WENDY... WE'RE COUNTING ON YOU... WE'LL TRY TO BE BACK BEFORE NIGHTTIME...

DON'T WORRY, MOM...

...I'VE GOT MY EYE ON THE HERD.

BYE! BYE!

MEUH

BUSTIER

AGAR

MMMAC

POC POC POC

CAZENOVE & WILLIAM

DIDN'T YOU BRING YOUR WATER BOTTLE, MAUREEN?!

TO DO WHAT WITH IT?

WELL, WHEN YOU PLAN ON TAKING A LONG WALK, IT'S ALWAYS A GOOD IDEA TO BRING SOMETHING TO DRINK.

MYUP... YOU KNOW, NAT, WE REALLY RAN AROUND A LOT WHEN WE WERE OUT WEST.

WE CROSSED BIG DESERTS FILLED WITH SAND...

AND WE WALKED ON TOP OF REALLY WARM BIG BOULDERS IN THE MIDDLE OF NOWHERE...

...1000 DEGREES, AT LEAST...

...AND I DIDN'T BRING MY WATER BOTTLE WITH ME ONCE.

WOW... YOU DON'T SAY! WHAT DID YOU DO WHEN YOU WERE THIRSTY?

THE SECRET IS TO LOCATE THE NEAREST WATER SOURCES.

YOU COULD FIND A WATER SOURCE HERE, TOO? JUST LIKE THAT?

PIECE OF CAKE!

GIVE ME YOUR WATER BOTTLE!

≈MWARF- ARF!≈

CAZENOVE & WILLIAM

TELL ME MORE ABOUT YOUR TRIP OUT WEST, WENDY...

FOR EXAMPLE, WHAT'S THE GRAND CANYON LIKE?

THERE REALLY AREN'T WORDS FOR IT. IT'S GINORMOUS...

...TOTALLY WILD.

OKAY, WHERE'S THE GRAND CANNON AT?

GIRLS, HERE'S MT. RUSHMORE, WITH FACES OF THE FIRST PRESIDENTS CARVED INTO THE ROCK.

THRUSH MORGUE? YUCK! THAT'S DISGUSTING!

I'VE WANTED TO SEE THE NEVADA DESERT FOR AGES!

DIDN'T SEE ANY NEIGH FODDER DESSERTS.

YOSEMITE PARK'S TOO BEAUTIFUL!

AH, NO—HEY! KEEP YOUR MITTS OFF MY T-SHIRT, YOU SANDY NITS.

PAT PAT
PAT
SMAK
PAT

EVERYTHING WAS GREAT, SAMMIE.

DID YOU LIKE IT, TOO, MAUREEN?

WELLLL...

UHMMM...I DON'T KNOW. NOT TOO MUCH...

BECAUSE I DIDN'T SEE ALL THAT... WE DIDN'T TAKE THE SAME TRIP...

??? WAAAAHH...

CAZENOVE & WILLIAM

ON VACATION, WE WENT TO A GREAT TOURIST ATTRACTION...

IT'S CALLED **MONSTERWORLD.**

I WANTED TO GO THERE WITH DADDY FIRST, CUZ I LOVE MONSTERS.

TOO CUTE!

GMAAAH...

BEUHAAH...

YIPPEE!... JUNGLE GIRL OF THE SAVANNAH SWINGS FROM VAMPIRE TO VAMPIRE...

RIIIPP

RRiipp

MWARF-ARF-AG! I LOOOOVE IT...

IT'S LIKE UNSPOOLING A BALL OF MOMMY'S YARN...

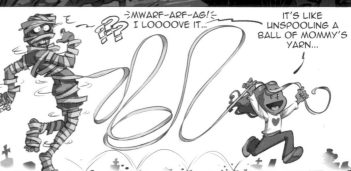

TCHAK

OCTOPUS SALAD FOR LUNCH WITH LOTS OF RUBBER THINGIES.

DID YOU GO TO "MONSTERWORLD"?

SEEMS FREAKY.

MYUP, MEH, S'ALRIGHT, KINDA RUNDOWN, EVEN DISAPPOINTING, YOU KNOW. THE COSTUMES WERE PRETTY AWFUL...

SNIF

GRUMBL

CAZENOVE & WILLIAM

TARGARYEN VESSEL PULVERIZED...

...DRAGON IN ITS NEST...

...MISSION ACCOMPL--

÷EEURRK!÷... SUPER HIT...

GAZZZ...

DON'T WORRY, EMMA...

IT'S MY SISTER'S GAME OF THE MOMENT.

GAZZZ.

SHE'S PLAYING THAT SHE'S BEEN PARALYZED BY AN EXTRATERRESTRIAL LASER BEAM.

UH-HUH. STILL INTO SPACE, YOUR SISTER.

GAZZZ...

SOMETIMES IT'S IN THE MIDDLE OF A MEAL...

GAZZZ.

IN THE MIDDLE OF THE ROAD, EVEN...

GAZZZ.

IT'S A GAME WITH OUR PARENTS...

AFTER FIVE MINUTES, MY MOTHER OR MY FATHER SAYS THE MAGIC THE WORLD...

...AND THAT FREES HER, GET IT?

BUT WHAT MAUREEN DOESN'T KNOW IS THAT THEY'VE LEFT TO GO SHOPPING NOW...

THEY'LL BE GONE FOR SEVERAL HOURS AT LEAST.

HA! HA! HA!

NWAAHH-HA HA!

AND THE MAGIC WORD?

CAZENOVE & WILLIAM

FOR EXAMPLE, THERE'S THE NIGHT WE WENT TO SEE THE BASKETBALL GAME...

...THAT MASON'S TEAM WON...

YYAAHAAAH!

IT WAS THE SAME THING WHEN SHE MADE TWO STRAYKES OR WHATEVER-THEY-ARE IN A ROW...

YAAHAAAH! YAAHAAAH!

STRIKE 2 3

2 STRIKE

OR WHEN SHE GOT AN EMAIL FROM HER NEW PEN PAL FROM THE U.K....

YAAHAAAH!

PONK

THE SAME THING WHEN WE BUMPED INTO *SAMAHA.* YOU KNOW, THE SINGER IN SHAKA PONK...

YAHAAAAH!

AND I WON'T EVEN TELL YOU ABOUT LAST NIGHT, WHEN DADDY AND MOMMY GAVE HER A PARAGLIDER FLIGHT AS A PRESENT FOR HER BIRTHDAY...

NO, I'M TELLING YOU... WHEN SHE SCREAMS LIKE THAT, SHE'S HAPPY.

YAAHAAAAHHH...AAI AAAH...AAI

YAAH...

CAZENOVE & WILLIAM

BRAVOOOO, SISTER!

YOU'RE SO THE BESSSSST!

YOU COULD HAVE EVEN FLOWN ALL THE WAY TO THE MOON...

SO HOW WAS THE PARAGLIDER FLIGHT, WENDY?

WOO, FAB! BUT MY LEGS ARE LIKE JELLY, I WON'T LIE...

MWAH-HA! NO, MAUREEN... LEGS LIKE JELLY IS AN EXPRESSION.

HA! HOPELESS!

THAT MEANS THAT--THAT-- IT'S ACTUALLY-- WHEN YOU--

IT'S HARD TO EXPLAIN IT, YOU KNOW.

HERE. SHOW ME THE VIDEO YOU MADE OF MY FLIGHT. I'LL SHOW YOU WHEN MY LEGS WERE LIKE JELLY.

OH, BUT I DIDN'T VIDEO IT WITH YOUR CELL PHONE.

I TOOK LOTS OF PHOTOS OF SHEEP, INSTEAD!

AND EVEN THREE BUTTERFLIES ZOOMING ALONG.

SOOO CUTE.

YOU DIDN'T RECORD IT WITH MY CELLPHONE?!

OH, YOU-- ...I'M GOING TO-- GRRR...

UH, MAUREEN...

DO YOU NOW KNOW WHAT IT FEELS LIKE TO HAVE LEGS LIKE JELLY?

73

CAZENOVE & WILLIAM

MMMWAH-HA-HA... YOU DID THE RIGHT THING SPENDING TWO HOURS STYLING YOUR HAIR, WENDY. HEE-HEE-HEE!

OUCH!

YOU'RE RIGHT! ∵UGH!∵

THIS CRAZY WIND. IT'S--

UH-OH. DID YOU SEE THAT, MAUREEN?

ALL THESE KITES... WOW!

THEY'RE SO BEAUTIFUL, THESE KIDDIE KITES.

LET'S MAKE ONE, WENDY!

FOR SURE! LET'S GET WHAT WE NEED AND MEET BACK IN THE GARDEN.

THAT'LL BE SOOO COOL!

AH! HERE'S A BALL OF STRING.

MAUREEN...

I'M READY...

OH, HELLO...

ME, TOO! I'M SUPER READY FOR TAKEOFF!

COME ON, COME ON! MAKE ME FLY!

CAZENOVE & WILLIAM

HOLD ON THERE...MISS POTIMARY...

...GET OVER HERE.

WHAT ARE THESE?

WELL... TOMATOES...

YES, BUT THESE ARE GREEN. YOU SHOULD NOT PICK THEM YET.

IT WAS TO MAKE YOU HAPPY.

I KNOW. I'M NOT BAWLING YOU OUT. IT'S JUST SO YOU KNOW HOW TO RECOGNIZE WHEN A TOMATO IS COMPLETELY RIPE.

LOOK!

YUMMM... CRUNCHY AND TENDER AT THE SAME TIME...

PROPERLY SOUR AND SWEET...

...WITH THIS BRIGHT COLOR...

...WHAT ELSE?

CHOMP CHOMP

AHA! I GET IT NOW!

THANKS, WENDY!

MY SISTER'S REALLY VERY SWEET, BUT...

I'VE HUGE DOUBTS SHE GOT IT!

DON'T WORRY. I'M NOT GOING TO PICK THESE. THEY AREN'T RIPE.

CRUNCH

I'LL COME BACK AGAIN AND CHECK TOMORROW.

CAZENOVE & WILLIAM

FWOOSH! FWOOSH! FWOOSH!

UHHHH... WHAT'S THAT WEIRD NOISE, WENDY?

OH, THAT?! MY SISTER'S NEW THING.

SHE IMITATES SOUNDS FROM EVERYDAY LIFE.

I GUESS THAT'S THE SOUND OF BRUSHING TEETH.

FWOOSH!

FWOOSH! FWOOSH!

AND IF I PUT SOME BREAD INTO THE TOASTER FOR US NOW?

PSHEEE...

CHTOOOOING!

DONE! THE TOAST IS READY.

I'M CLIMBING UP THE STAIRS NOW...

PATOOM! PATOOM! PATOOM! PATOOM! PATOOM! PATOOM!...

AWW!... I LOVE IT!

≥SIGH.≤... IT GOES ON FOR HOURS LIKE THIS...

SHE DOESN'T KNOW WHEN TO STOP.

...OH, HERE! IF I OPENED THE DOOR TO WENDY'S ROOM...

SSQQUEEEEK! WHOA THERE, GOODNESS GRACIOUS. IT NEEDS OILING.

PFFF...

AND THERE, THAT'S THE SOUND AS IF I WERE RUMMAGING THROUGH HER THINGS...

HA-HA, I'M A FAN!

RUMMAGE

RUMMAGE

RUMMAGE?

OOOH! THAT LITTLE PEST!

CALM DOWN, WENDY.

NO, NO, CALM DOWN!

AGRRR.

≥AGRRR≤... I KNOW HOW TO MAKE THE NOISE OF WALLOPING YOU! WANT TO HEAR?!

CAZENOVE & WILLIAM

THROW A DART AND PICK ONE. IT'LL BE FINE.

OH, NO! ABSOLUTELY NOT...

I WANT TO FIND THE ONE THAT WILL MAKE HER JUMP WITH JOY.

IT'S FOR HER BIRTHDAY, YOU KNOW.

HMM...

GET THIS ONE. IT'S SUPER TRENDY.

MY LITTLE COUSIN WON'T LET GO OF HERS. SHE'S NUTS ABOUT IT.

OR THIS ONE... LISTEN TO THE RACKET IT MAKES.

HONK HONK

HONK HONK HONK

LOL! YOU'RE MENTAL, MASE!

HA! HA!

THEY'LL HAVE THAT IN COMMON.

I FOUND IT! IT'S PERFECT! GRAB THAT BOX UP THERE FOR ME, PLEASE.

YUCK! IT'S REALLY HIDEOUS!

IT'S ALL SCRAWNY. ARE YOU SURE ABOUT THIS, WENDY?

GUARANTEED SUCCESS, I'M TELLING YOU...

WAYAAAAH! I LOVE IT! I LOVE IT!

SO PRETTY!

PLUS, I DIDN'T HAVE THIS BOX...

WHEN I TELL YOU I KNOW, IT'S BECAUSE I KNOW.

THANKS, WENDY!

CAZENOVE & WILLIAM

I'VE SPENT DAYS GETTING READY...

SQUEEEK

SNOOORE
ZZZZZZ
SN--

FIRST WAITING UNTIL MY SISTER'S ASLEEP TO GO IN HER ROOM...

SNOOORE
PSSHHHZZZ

SNOOORE

ACTING LIKE I'M SLEEPWALKING...

AND STEALING HER PRIVATE DIARY.

ZZZ

I KNEW THIS WAS SUCCCHH A GREAT IDEA!

YES!

SQUEEEEK

CLIK

PROOF THAT IT WAS A GOOD IDEA.

ZZZ ZZZ
ZZZ...

...WENDY STOLE IT FROM ME.

ZZ ZZZ...

CAZENOVE & WILLIAM

MY SISTER AND I LOVE INVENTING NEW SPORTS...

LIKE *ROLLERTON*...

BADMINTON AND ROLLERBLADING. IT'S THE BEST!

TUNK

RRRRRRROOUL...

WE ALSO INVENTED *BASKALONGJUMP*.

WENDY'S THE BEST AT IT, BUT THAT'S BECAUSE SHE'S TALL LIKE A BEANPOLE.

DUNK DUNK

YEEHAAAH!

PHHOOEY... YOU'RE A REAL KANGAROO. IT'S NOT FAIR!

MY FAVORITE OF ALL IS *ARCHERPONG*...

WOO-HOOOO! THREE POINTS FOR SITTING MAUREEN!

TOK

WENDY, WHAT COULD WE MIX WITH SWINGS?

HMM...

?!

HEY, GIRLS... HAVE YOU FINISHED YOUR HOMEWORK FOR TOMORROW?

RRRO RR RRR RRO O

YEAH, WELL, *"REVIEWSWING"* IS A ROTTEN SPORT!

YUP! THE LAMEST OF LAME!

RRR... RROO RRR

CAZENOVE & WILLIAM

MMM... A... A... AAA...

?!

CHOOO!

MUNCH YUM! MUNCH MUNCH MMM...

GULP?!

COFF KUH R KUH RR KUH KOUGH KOUGH KOUGH KUH KUHAAR RR KUH KU KOUGH RR R RR KOUGH KOUGH RR KOUGH

BRRR! BRRR! BRRR!

BRRR BRRR BRRR!

SNURF SNURF

NOM NOM SNARF SNARF GURGL SLURP! PROUITCH! PROUITCH! PROUITCH!

HUMPF!

UH, YES, MAUREEN...

I REMEMBER THOSE TIMES VERY WELL.

YOU'RE NOT GOING TO SCARE ME WITH YOUR ZOMBIE COSTUME.

I'M IMMUNE.

CAZENOVE & WILLIAM

TONY, TONY! WAIT!

SAY, WOULD YOU LIKE TO CARRY MY BACKPACK, PRETTY PLEASE? IT'S TOO HEAVY FOR MY LI'L ARMS.

UH... AH... OKAY...

HEY, MAUREEN! YOU DIDN'T LISTEN CAREFULLY TO WHAT THE TEACHER TOLD US!

WHEN SHE TALKED ABOUT RECESS AND SNACK TIME?!

NO. WHEN SHE DID THE CLASS WITH US ABOUT EQUALITY.

JUST NOW. IT WAS LESS THAN AN HOUR AGO.

HMM...

WHEN SHE EXPLAINED THAT WE'RE ALL EQUAL ON THIS EARTH...

NO MORE DIFFERENCES. ALL THAT...

AH, YESSS... I'VE ALREADY FORGOTTEN.

THAT'S RIGHT! SINCE WE'RE ALL EQUAL...

...THAT MEANS THERE'S NO REASON FOR ME TO HOLD YOUR BACKPACK, MAUREEN.

YOU DIDN'T UNDERSTAND ANYTHING! IT'S ONLY AMONG GIRLS THAT EVERYONE'S EQUAL!

IF HE CARRIES YOUR BACKPACK, MAUREEN, HE HAS TO CARRY OURS.

YEP, NAT! THAT'S EQUALITY!

HA! HA!

HEE-HEE!

MUARF!

CAZENOVE & WILLIAM

WE'VE NEVER THOUGHT OF PLAYING AT DOING VOICES FOR A TV SERIES BEFORE!

WITH THE MICS FROM YOUR NINTENDOX, IT'LL BE LIKE FOR REAL.

WE'LL LEAN ON THIS TO READ OUR SCRIPTS.

OH, YESSS.... LIKE THE TV NEWS.

I'LL DO THE VOICE OF *KELLY*, PRETEEN IN LOVE WHO ASKS WAY TOO MANY QUESTIONS.

HEE-HEE-HEE!

I'M *ASHLEE*. I SING THE THEME SONG AND TELL THE STORY OF MY FRIENDS *DOROTHY* AND *NATALIE*.

THEY SAY VOICE-HOOVER.

NO, IT'S VOICE-OVER.

WHO WILL YOU BE NOW, LULU?

MANNY, BECAUSE I CAN MIMIC BOY'S LOW VOICES REALLY WELL.

FIVE MINUTES LATER...

YUP...

OKAY...

≥PHEWW!≤ ...TAKING LONG!

COME ON ALREADYYYY, EH.... BILL AND COO LIKE USUAL.

WELL, YEAH. IF YOU DON'T MOVE YOUR LIPS, HOW DO YOU EXPECT US TO DUB OUR VOICES IN?!

CAZENOVE & WILLIAM

SAMMIE, GIVE ME TWO OR THREE WORDS...

...JUST LIKE THAT, WITHOUT THINKING.

WELL, BARSTOOL, CARNIVAL, AND RATAFIOLE.

RATAFIOLE, ⇒PFF!⇐... HA-HA... WHATEVS!

I'LL ADD GRAPNEL, COYOTE AND TURTLE TREE.

NOW COUNTRIES: PARAGUAY, CHILE, AND CAMEROON...

LAPLAND, MEXICO...

POLAND...

ADD THE RECIPE FOR SAMOSAS, CHOCOLATE, ROQUEFORT...

I KNOW THE ONE FOR RATATOUILLE, IF YOU'D LIKE.

AND THERE WE GO! I'LL PUT MY PRIVATE DIARY BACK INTO ITS SPOT.

FOLLOW ME.

WE'LL HIDE AND WAIT...

TURTLE TREE?

RATAFIOLE, RATA... RATATOU?

HAS MY SISTER BLOWN A FUSE, OR WHAT?

IT'S GOT TO BE A SECRET CODE.

YES, WE HAVE TO CRACK IT...

THE IDEA OF A FAKE DIARY'S TOTALLY WILD!

CAZENOVE & WILLIAM

WENDY, WENDY, WENDY...

WILL YOU GET IN THE BATHTUB WITH ME? I PUT IN LOTS OF BUBBLES.

WAIT, DID YOU TAKE ME FOR A BABY OR WHAT?!

HA HA HA

HEE HEE HEE

BUT... THE WATER'S HOT, JUST THE WAY YOU LIKE IT.

SAMMIE, EMMA, AND I ARE TALKING ABOUT BIG GIRL THINGS, YOU KNOW.

BUT--

GO, SCAT! VAMOOSE!

HA! HA!

HEE-HEE!

TAKE YOUR TOYS AND YOUR STUFFED ANIMALS IF YOU'RE AFRAID OF BEING ALONE IN THE TUB.

HONESTLY, WHAT A LITTLE BABY!

≥PFFF!≤... I COULDN'T CARE LESS, YOU OLD BANANA PEEL!

HA! HA!
HA! HA!
HEE!
HEE!
HEE!

I DON'T NEED HER ANYWAY..

UH, OH! GRODZILLA'S COMING OUT OF HIS LAIR...

WHILE THE TIPANIC'S HEADED RIGHT AT HIM.

QUIIIICK. THE LIFE PRESERVERS. QUIIIICK...

...WOMEN AND CHILDREN FIRST...

OOOH!... BUT THE TIPANIC CAN FLY. WOW!... CRODZILLA FLIES, TOO.

SPLASH

?

HEE-HEE... UHHH... MY PALS JUST LEFT.

CAZENOVE & WILLIAM

85

HEY, SAMMIE, DID YOU NOTICE ANYTHING ABOUT WENDY?

YEP! I THINK I KNOW WHAT YOU'RE TALKING ABOUT.

NOT TOO LONG AGO, SHE WENT PARAGLIDING...

COME OVER HERE... CLOSER, CLOSER. I'M CHECKING!

SHE LOVES BUNGEE JUMPING...

SMILE, GIRLS. YOU'RE ON CAMERA.

WHEEEE!

THE HIGH ROPES COURSE AT LEAST ONCE A MONTH.

OOyOOOyOOOyOOO...

HEEEY... I'M THE ONE WHO DOES JUNGLE GIRL OF THE SAVANNAH. COPYCAT!

SHE TOOK A SKYDIVING CLASS.

NO, WENDY... YOU DON'T GO BY YOURSELF DURING THE FIRST LESSON!

÷MWARF!÷ I COULDN'T CARE LESS! I'M NOT EVEN SCARED!

RRROO...

FREE FALL

F-GJBP

SHE'S A THRILLSEEKER AND LIKES HER THRILLS BIGGER AND BIGGER.

TOTALLY!

THAT'S WHY SHE SUGGESTED TO HER PARENTS THAT SHE'D WATCH MAUREEN AND HER BUDDIES FOR THEIR PAJAMA PARTY...

COMPARED TO THAT, SKYDIVING'S A WALK IN THE PARK!

BOING
BOING
BOING

CAZENOVE & WILLIAM

UH, OH... A BIG VILLAIN WANTS TO HIT A LITTLE KID...

IT LOOKS LIKE HE WANTS TO TAKE HIS LUNCH MONEY...

NO! NO! DON'T HIT ME, DON'T HIT ME...

THE BIG GLASSES INTO THE GARBAGE CAN...

THEY'RE TOO UGLY, PBESIDES...

SHE LOOKS BETTER WITHOUT THEM.

...YIKES... OOOH, NOOO...

SHE SPINS...

BRAKWPOW

...HOLY COW, WOO-HOO, MY MY...

TADAAH!

I FEEL DIZZY...

YIKES...WHA... HOW MANY...TURNS DOES WONDER WOMAN MAKE?

WOOHO

I DON'T KNOW... BUT YOU CAN'T WALK STRAIGHT AFTERWARDS... →WHEW!←...

WHEW...

WANT TO THROW UP...

???

CAZENOVE & WILLIAM

IF THERE'S ONE PERSON WHO LIKES TO MAKE LIFE COMPLICATED, IT'S REALLY MAUREEN.

NAH NAH NAH... I'M NOT JUST GOING TO DRAW... THAT'D BE TOO EASY-PEASY.

I'VE CREATED A GREAT GAME WHERE YOU HAVE TO DRAW BLINDFOLDED.

YOU'LL ONLY SEE THE RESULTS AT THE END...

...SAME AS ME.

FIRST, I SPIN IN PLACE, LIKE THIS...

AT LEAST TEN TURNS!

ONE, TWO, THREE, FOUR, FIVE...

HUH... HUH... WHERE ARE THE FELT TIP PENS?

AH! HERE THEY ARE!

WOO! HA-HA!

OFF WE GO! I'M CREATIONING TO THE MAX.

SQUEE SQUEEK SQUEE

GESTURES FULL OF ENERGY...

THAT'S ART!

SWIP SWIP swip SWIP SWIP

BACKWARDS...

WITH BOTH HANDS AT THE SAME TIME.

SWIP SWIP swip

IT'S GOING TO BE SUPER EXTRA PRETTY!

NOTHING?

??? ??

MY FELT TIP PENS DON'T WORK OR WHAT?!

OOOH, YES! THEY ACTUALLY WORK VERY, VERY WELL.

AGRRR...

GULP!

HUMPF

GRUMPF

CAZENOVE & WILLIAM

WOOOW... YOU'VE REALLY GOT "SUPER FRUTOX" BOTTLE CAPS!

WELL, I EVEN HAVE THREE ADAM APPLES, PLUS TWO LEON LEMONS AND ABBY PRICOT.

YOU EVEN HAVE "PETER PLUM," WHICH IS REALLY, REALLY RARE...

BUT I DON'T YET HAVE PINA APPLE OR PENELOPE NUT.

SO, I STOPPED! RIGHT AWAY!

IT'S LIKE THESE INDESTRUC-TIBLES FIGURES...

...YOU HAVE ALMOST THE WHOLE COLLECTION.

ELASTIGIRL AND EVIL SYNDROME ARE UNFINDERABLE.

OLD MAID PLAYING CARDS WITH PHOTOS OF DOGS ON THEM, YOU KNOW?

I THOUGHT I COULD FINISH THOSE...

...THEY PUT A CARD IN EACH CONTAINER OF YOGURT. BUT THEY STOPPED.

PLUS THEIR YOGURT'S DISGUSTING!

AS A RESULT, YOU'VE GOT LOTS OF COLLECTIONS, BUT NONE IS COMPLETE.

OH, YES, I DO! I'VE GOT ONE!

MY SISTER COLLECTION! THIS ONE'S COMPLETE!

CAZENOVE & WILLIAM

MAUREEN!

FOR HEAVEN'S SAKE! WHAT ARE YOU DOING?

YOU'RE A REAL NITWIT! ONLY THE FOOD IS SELF-SERVE.

YEAH, WELL, THEY DIDN'T EXPLAIN THINGS VERY WELL.

UH... I'M REALLY VERY SORRY...

CAZENOVE & WILLIAM

LOOK AT HOW PRETTY THIS IS.

IT WAS GOOD WE CAME HERE.

THIS SPOT IS SSOOO CUTE!

PRESTO! PHOTO SOUVENIR!

A LI'L SMILE, MAUREEN...

CHEEEESE!

DO YOU THINK WE CAN VISIT THAT VIADUCT OVER THERE?

I DON'T KNOW. WE SHOULD ASK SOMEONE.

PLUS WE HAVE TO GET LOTS OF POST-CARDS...

PINS...

MAGNETS...

SNOW GLOBES...

UUHH... WHAT'S GOTTEN INTO YOU?

YOU GREW UP HERE, DIDN'T YOU?

YES, SAMMIE, BUT WE'RE PRACTICING FOR OUR FUTURE WORK WHEN WE GROW UP.

WE'RE GOING TO START OUR OWN COMPANY!

WHAT KIND OF COMPANY?

PROFESSIONAL TOURISTS!

BUT ⇒PHEW!⇐... IT'S A LOT OF WORK!

CAZENOVE & WILLIAM

REMEMBER, MAUREEN...

...IT WAS A BLAST...

AFTER YOUR FIRST HALLOWEEN, YOU DIDN'T WANT TO MISS A SINGLE THING.

AH, BUT I OBVIOUSLY LOVED IT!

YOU WENT TO GET CANDY FROM THE NEIGHBORS UNTIL YOU WERE HOW OLD, MAUREEN?

JEEZ, I CAN'T REMEMBER ANY LONGER.

BUT IT'S ALL GOOD... I'M PAST THE AGE FOR GOING TO GET CANDY FROM FOLKS.

DING DONG

SLURP

AH! SPEAK OF THE DEVIL...

DIIING... DOOOONG.

YES... YESSS... JUST A MINUTE...

HERE, I'M COMING!

BOOO!

HURK HURK HURK

AAAAAH

NOWADAYS I PREFER TO GET IT DELIVERED!

YUMMY! WANT SOME?

CAZENOVE & WILLIAM

WATCH OUT FOR PAPERCUTZ™

Welcome to the slightly sentimental, super-scenic sixth THE SISTERS graphic novel, "Hurricane Maureen," by Christophe Cazenove, writer, and William Maury, artist, from Papercutz, those tree-hugging types dedicated to publishing great graphic novels for all ages. I'm Jim Salicrup, Editor-in-Chief and Secret Gardener, here with some thoughts regarding THE SISTERS and another Papercutz graphic novel or two that are sure to excite you…

In THE SISTERS we often get to see the super-heroic fantasy life of Wendy and Maureen as they interact with super-villains and gigantic monsters, having wild adventures that are based on their imaginative re-shaping of everyday ordinary life. These fun-filled flights of fantasy have proven so popular that we recently released THE SUPER SISTERS, an entire graphic novel filled with expanded versions of Wendy

and Maureen's imaginary exploits. THE SUPER SISTERS has proven to be a big hit as well, but some of you have responded by saying that as much as they love Wendy and Maureen's pretend exploits, that they'd love to see some real super-powered kids. Well, your wish is our command, so allow me to introduce you to an all-new series from Papercutz… THE MYTHICS.

As the title implies, the series is based on mythology. And although the lead characters are also modern kids, instead of having imaginary adventures, they're having to right now confront very real challenges that originated way back in the mythological past. In THE MYTHICS #1 "Heroes Reborn," we meet the modern-day ancestors of three ancient gods, who get handed down great powers. It all begins when…

The god of lightning, Raijin, instills his powers in Yuko, a Japanese schoolgirl in a rock band. Yuko must learn to wield her newfound electrical powers to defeat Fuijin, the evil god of wind, before he destroys all of Japan.

Meanwhile, in Egypt, young Amir, a recently orphaned boy taking over his father's successful company and landholdings, encounters Horus, the Sun and Moon god. Horus and Amir must stop evil, in the form of Seth, from reanimating all the dead mummies and taking over the world.

Lastly, a young opera hopeful, Abigail, must face a blizzard freezing all of Germany orchestrated by Loki, the evil god of mischief. Under the guidance of Freyja, the Norse god of beauty, Abigail must find her voice and her mythic weapon to stop evil in its tracks. And that's just the beginning, in THE MYTHICS #2 "Apocalypse Ahead," we'll meet three more ancestors of the old gods as they join the fight against ancient evil. The premiere volume of THE MYTHICS is available now at booksellers and libraries everywhere.

Of course, for those of you who prefer more true-to-life stories, may we suggest DANCE CLASS? This series features the earth-bound Julie (and her younger sister, Capucine), Alia, and Lucie, but when they dance, it's almost as if they're defying gravity. Most DANCE CLASS graphic novels feature the girls getting ready to put on a big show, and in DANCE CLASS #10 "Letting It Go,"by Béka and Crip, they're rehearsing for a production of "The Snow Queen," but an awesome dress that was created for the star of the show suddenly disappears, causing all sorts of trouble. See for yourself in the special preview on the following pages…

As for Wendy and Maureen, aside from THE SUPER SISTERS #1, they'll be back in the next THE SISTERS graphic novel coming soon. You don't want to miss it!

Thanks,

Jim

STAY IN TOUCH!

EMAIL: salicrup@papercutz.com
WEB: www.papercutz.com
TWITTER: @papercutzgn
INSTAGRAM: @papercutzgn
FACEBOOK: PAPERCUTZGRAPHICNOVELS
REGULAR MAIL: Papercutz, 160 Broadway, Suite 700, East Wing, New York, NY 10038

Here's a special preview of DANCE CLASS #10 "Letting it Go"…

WHAT'S GOING ON, **CAPUCINE?** SOMETHING BOTHERING YOU?

I DIDN'T DANCE TODAY!

CLIC

OH? ME EITHER. THAT HAPPENS SOMETIMES...

IN MY BOOK, THEY SAY THAT TO BECOME A PRIMA BALLERINA, YOU HAVE TO DANCE EVERY DAY!

HMMM. THAT'S TRUE.

OKAY. IT'S NOT MIDNIGHT YET!

AND?

WE CAN STILL DANCE BEFORE TOMORROW. COME ON, CAPUCINE!

POF POF POF POF POF POF

POF POF POF POF POF POF

POF POF POF

DO YOU HEAR THAT NOISE?

IT'S NOTHING. YOU HAVE THE GIRLS ON YOUR MIND. GO BACK TO SLEEP.

12:03

Don't miss DANCE CLASS #10 "Letting It Go" available now wherever books are sold!